TWIST OF FATE
A Love Story

ANNA REILLY

Anna Reilly

Copyright © 2017 Anna Reilly
All rights reserved.

Book cover design by SelfPubBookCovers.com/Daniela

ISBN-10: 1544816979
ISBN-13: 9781544816975

ANNA REILLY is blessed to live in Newfoundland, Canada with her talented and witty husband of more than 20 years. One of her greatest joys is witnessing her extraordinary son pursue his own dreams. Anna is a business professional by day and a writer at night. She has a BA in English Literature from Memorial University of Newfoundland and an MBA from the University of Leicester in England. TWIST OF FATE is her first novel.

Anna would love to hear from you! Visit her website www.annareilly.ca or write to her at anna@annareilly.ca.

ACKNOWLEDGEMENTS

Thank you to the talented authors of Romancing the Rock for hosting the EXPOsed Conference in September 2016. Your willingness to share your knowledge and experiences was inspiring. I left the event feeling empowered and determined to write and publish a book. And here I am. Thank you to the local authors (especially Candace and Kate) who answered my questions and provided encouragement these past few weeks; you kindly helped me navigate these unfamiliar waters of independent publishing.

Derek - Merci for providing insight into policing matters referenced in this story. Any errors or misrepresentations are mine!

Ted - Thank you for suggesting the title for the book. I was stuck and you saved the day! Squirrel!

Leeland - Love and gratitude for helping me work through the logistics of this story idea. You are a fabulous sounding board and a phenomenal partner in life!

Lori-Ann, Judy, Ted, Cindy, Heidi, Camille, Charlene, Marguerite, Vanessa and Derek - Deep appreciation to my early readers for your invaluable feedback and suggestions. And for your encouragement!! Special thanks to my sister-in-law Lori-Ann for being my unofficial editor. I look forward to returning the favour one day soon!

Leeland, Riley and Mom (the best for last) - Heartfelt thanks and love to the loves of my life for always believing in me and enduring my endless chatter about this project. Your support and encouragement make every day extraordinary and no dream too far out of reach. I am blessed and grateful.

For Dad. I miss you every day. I hope you somehow know my dreams are coming true.

CONTENTS

CHAPTER 1 1
CHAPTER 2 10
CHAPTER 3 14
CHAPTER 4 21
CHAPTER 5 30
CHAPTER 6 36
CHAPTER 7 41
CHAPTER 8 48
CHAPTER 9 56
CHAPTER 10 64
CHAPTER 11 72
CHAPTER 12 79
CHAPTER 13 82
CHAPTER 14 88
CHAPTER 15 95
CHAPTER 16 99
CHAPTER 17 106
CHAPTER 18 115
CHAPTER 19 121

CHAPTER 20	124
CHAPTER 21	131
CHAPTER 22	137
CHAPTER 23	146
CHAPTER 24	149
CHAPTER 25	159
CHAPTER 26	166
CHAPTER 27	174
CHAPTER 28	179
CHAPTER 29	185
CHAPTER 30	194
CHAPTER 31	198
CHAPTER 32	205
CHAPTER 33	212
CHAPTER 34	217
CHAPTER 35	220
EPILOGUE	228

CHAPTER 1

Alyson stifled the scream that tore through her chest and threatened to disrupt the stillness of the surrounding forest. She stopped dead in her tracks, almost losing her footing on the uneven terrain and quickly grabbed at a nearby branch to maintain her balance. There was a man standing less than ten feet from her. She had no warning at all that he was there until she glanced up and saw him, standing completely still, watching her. He was a hulking, unkempt presence in her otherwise tranquil morning hike. He looked disheveled and grubby and she couldn't imagine what he was doing roaming these woods in the middle of November. Probably nothing good. He was carrying a huge backpack, the kind that mountain climbers and hikers carry on long treks. He was dressed in what looked like army surplus clothing; an oversized khaki parka, canvas pants and battered hiking boots. His clothing looked worn and in desperate need of a laundromat or trash bin. His face was concealed behind a thick, black beard and he wore a dark knit hat, pulled low over his forehead.

The fleeting impression that he looked almost as startled as she felt did little to comfort her. He seemed glued to the spot, warily watching her, presumably to see what she might do next. She wasn't sure what to do. She had never encountered people in these woods before. The trails were seldom used and didn't form part of the popular coastal trail system. Her heart was pounding so fast she could feel it throbbing in her head. The roar of blood coursing through her veins was deafening as it pulsated in her ears.

She figured she had two options. She could continue hiking or turn around and run like hell back to her house. If she walked past him she would be walking even deeper into the woods and she was already at least two kilometers from home. Plus she really didn't want to get that close to him. The path was narrow and he was big. If she turned back she would be walking in the same direction as him and he could potentially follow her right to her doorstep. She sincerely doubted that she could outrun him. She didn't want him knowing where she lived.

For the first time since moving here, she regretted that she hadn't made friends in the area. No one knew where she was this morning. No one would miss her or know she was gone, not until her family or best friend tried to reach her. That might be days from now. She was a loner by choice and now she was alone with a stranger who might be harmless or any number of horrible, terrifying things. She had no way of knowing.

She decided to pass by him and keep hiking, even though she had been planning to turn back soon. There was a storm forecasted to hit later that day and the meteorologists were warning it was going to be nasty, bringing heavy snow and winds, creating whiteout conditions that could last for days. She did not want to get caught in that mess. She figured if she walked for another twenty minutes and then trekked back, there'd be enough distance between her and the stranger by then that she would be safe. *Unless he followed her deeper into the woods.* The thought slammed into her and made her shiver as an icy rivulet of fear raced down her spine.

She moved forward slowly but steadily, keeping her eyes on the stranger except for the occasional glance down at the forest floor every few steps to ensure she didn't trip on the root of a tree. He didn't move, just stood silently watching her as she edged toward him. As she got closer she was startled to notice that he seemed every bit as unnerved as she was feeling.

"Excuse me," she murmured, her voice barely more than a squeak as she passed by him, their coats brushing on the narrow trail.

"Ma'am," was his gruff reply, his voice deep and rusty as though unused for a long time.

He was bigger than she initially thought, at least six feet in height and while he didn't smell as bad as she had expected, he did emanate a discernable odour of neglect. He definitely had been nowhere near a washing machine or shower in the past few weeks. Again she wondered what he was doing in the backwoods of Newfoundland on the precipice of winter. No one in their right mind would camp in these forests this late in the season, assuming he was camping. He certainly didn't belong to her neighbourhood. She hadn't made much of an effort to meet the neighbours in the past eight months since moving here, but she knew it was an affluent area and many of the residents were doctors, lawyers and business professionals. All had access to indoor plumbing.

She glanced back over her shoulder to see if he was following her. He was still standing in the same spot but had turned and was watching her walk away. She picked up her pace and hurriedly put distance between them, not slowing until she had scaled a large hill and could see that he had not followed her. She paused for a moment to catch her breath and continued at a more moderate pace. She hoped she had made the right decision choosing to walk deeper into the forest. The nagging reminder that she was actually walking further away from help should she need it kept reverberating in her brain.

She also prayed that he wasn't lurking somewhere nearby waiting for her to turn back. If he meant her any harm he probably would have done something by now. A twinge of guilt emerged from the blanket of fear, and she silently berated herself for judging him based on his appearance. She didn't know his story. He might simply be down on his luck with no one to offer a hand back up. Regardless, when she noticed the broken branch a few feet ahead she picked it up. It wasn't much of a weapon but it was better than nothing at all.

She pushed the stranger from her mind and inevitably Joe, her beloved late husband, slipped into her thoughts, the only place where he still lived. He was the reason she had moved across the country from British Columbia to this little town on the northern tip of Newfoundland's Avalon Peninsula. Her family and friends, though well-meaning, had been driving her to the brink of madness with their unsolicited advice that it was time to move on, time to start dating again. They didn't understand. There was no one else for her. Joe was her one and only. She had never believed in the soul-mate nonsense or the concept of true love. Until she met Joe. The way she felt about him changed the way she felt about everything. No one had ever loved her like Joe. No one ever would. They had created amazing memories in their six short years together. Losing him had been the most difficult thing she had ever experienced. She almost hadn't survived it and many days she had sought the refuge of her bed. Sometimes she prayed that she would die too but her prayers went unanswered. The sun kept rising and setting to mark the passing of time. Here she was, still living, even if she was a shell of her former self.

She could recall every detail of the day he had been killed. She had gotten home from work first as she usually did and popped a chicken in the oven. She had been placing plates on the table of their uptown condo when the doorbell rang. In retrospect, there had been no ominous tone to the peal of the bell. Even when she opened the door to find two police officers standing on her doorstep, she hadn't thought to feel panicked or alarmed. When they asked her to confirm she was Alyson Fisher she calmly nodded in the affirmative. Whey they asked if they could come in, she stepped aside allowing them to walk past her into the small entryway of her condo. She remembered them removing their hats and shuffling their feet. They didn't quite make eye contact with her. Then they spoke the words that she had known were coming but didn't want to hear. Joe had been hit broadside by another driver. A drunk driver she would learn later. She heard the words and on some level she understood what they meant. Yet she stood in her front hallway blankly staring at them, remotely detached. She could remember being transfixed by the up and down movement of the younger officer's Adam's apple as he fought to contain his emotions while the senior officer, with regret, told her of her husband's death. Her Joe. Gone. Her first rational thought was to usher them out of her home and close the door. Reset. Make them go away and make the bad news somehow undo itself. She may have even said so out loud. She wasn't aware that tears were falling, her own tears, until the young officer placed his hand lightly on her shoulder in an awkward attempt to comfort her. He was losing the battle to keep his own emotions at bay and that made her feel marginally less alone in the shock of the horrible news still trying to process in her brain.

    She stupidly thought of the chicken. Who would eat it now? She thought of the plans they had made for the coming weekend; they had booked a cottage in the mountains and were going to rent kayaks and hike in the sunshine and make love under the stars. She'd have to cancel. She'd probably lose the deposit. She thought of the thousand mundane little things, to avoid thinking of the overwhelming truth. Her new truth. Life without Joe.

The hours and days immediately following his death were a blur of muddled, disjointed moments. Parents, her sister, relatives from both her and Joe's side of the family filled her small condo. It was suffocating and reassuring in equal measure. When the blessed numbness of the shock wore away, disbelief, anger and grief swallowed her whole and flattened her. She spent many of those early days sedated, caught in some hazy otherworld where the lines between reality and fantasy were completely obscured. Joe still existed in that pseudo-dream-world. She wanted to stay there with him forever.

But the living must live, or so she was repeatedly told, and slowly her persistent family and friends pulled her back into the light. Into the pain. Into the oppressive fear and sadness of existing in a world without Joe. She started seeing a therapist. She enrolled in grief counseling. She returned to her job as an editor with a large publishing house. But nothing had meaning. The condo was no longer a home; it was a constant reminder of all that was lost. She couldn't focus at work. She didn't want to socialize or spend time with anyone who wasn't Joe. She tried for almost a year to go through the motions of the life they had built together in Vancouver. It simply didn't work without him. Her life as she knew it was over. She had to get out of the condo and Vancouver. She felt strongly that the only thing that would help her, the only chance she had to start fresh was to make a radical change. Against the advice of her family, friends and therapist, she sold the condo and moved five thousand kilometers east to rural Newfoundland.

She chose Newfoundland based on a feeling. She had stumbled across a tourism ad online showcasing the whimsy of brightly coloured houses set against wind swept shorelines. That ad spoke to her. Everyone thought she was mad to move so far away and perhaps it wasn't the most well thought out decision she had ever made, but it *felt* right. Her gut was telling her to go. It was the first time she had felt hopeful since Joe had died.

She made the move completely on her own, refusing help from her parents and her sister Sydney. Her best friend Lois had begged to go with her to find a house and get settled, but Alyson was firm in her resolve to take care of everything herself. She loved her family. She loved Lois. But she couldn't breathe around them. They looked at her with so much hope and expectation and she was tired of disappointing them. On some level she knew she was being selfish. She knew that she was being cruel. For the preservation of her own sanity she needed the time and distance from those who loved her. She also knew none of them would approve of the choices she was about to make. They would expect her to choose the security and convenience of a condo in the city. That was the last thing she wanted. She craved windswept shorelines.

She arrived in Newfoundland early spring and stayed in a cozy bed and breakfast in downtown St. John's for the first few weeks. She had looked at several houses in the city but as charmed as she was by the seaside capital that melded centuries old architecture with cutting edge modern design, she simply didn't want to be surrounded by people. She asked her realtor to check for places outside the city. She found the perfect spot just north of St. John's. It was a big house for one person but she loved the country setting and the remoteness of the location. The house was a mere twenty-minute drive from the east end of St. John's but she felt as though she was in the middle of some vast wilderness.

Her new home was built on a small cliff overlooking the ocean with forest on the north side. The shoreline she had lusted after was virtually in her backyard. She had to compromise on the brightly coloured clapboard though. Her new abode was an uninspired charcoal grey with lighter grey brick detailing. Perhaps she'd change that in a few years. Her nearest neighbour was at least a kilometer away and her house was the last one on the narrow country road. The hustle and bustle of city life didn't reach into her small corner of the world jutting into the North Atlantic. The second story master bedroom, located at the rear of the house, had a private deck with a spectacular ocean view. It was her favourite spot in the house to watch the sun sinking into the sea every night. Everything about it was perfect. She had craved solitude and isolation; now she had both. Though in this moment she questioned the sanity of her decision. What if that stranger had been intent on harming her in some way? She would have been completely at his mercy. The thought frightened her.

She grunted as she realized that she actually felt fear for her safety and well-being. That was new. She had spent so much time wishing she had died along with Joe that she felt a bit gob smacked to realize she *did* care about waking up tomorrow. On the darkest days since losing Joe she had thought about how easy it would have been to take a handful of pills, go to sleep and never wake up. But then she'd think of her parents and Syd and Lois. Following that path would have destroyed them and even she wasn't selfish enough to hurt them like that. She also knew that Joe would be disappointed in her giving up on life if he could see her from some afterworld. He would be sad to see how withdrawn she had become, how isolated. How bitter. He would have wanted her to live. She knew that; she'd always known that. He would want her to not simply exist, as she had been these past two years since his death; no, he would want her to do something with her life. Something meaningful. He would want her to thrive. She felt a pang of sadness that he would never hold her in his arms again. And she felt shame at the thought that seeing her hollow life would disappoint him. She quietly resolved to try harder. To make a friend. To sign up for a class in art or photography or cooking. To find a part-time job or volunteer. Maybe she would get a dog, a companion and protector.

A surge of emotion pushed through her. She raised her face toward the sky and let her tears mix with the fat snowflakes that were falling all around her. It was time to go back home. Not to Vancouver but to the new home she had made in this windswept, rugged land that often felt like it was perched on the edge of the earth. It was time to find a purpose. She dabbed at her eyes and cheeks with her wool mittens and glanced at her watch. Twenty-two minutes had elapsed since her encounter with the stranger. It should be safe to go back now. She carefully picked her steps as the falling snow quickly transformed her world into a postcard worthy winter wonderland. She felt the tug of a smile lift the corners of her mouth as she deeply inhaled the earthy scent of pine and conifers mixing with the frosty air.

CHAPTER 2

John stood staring after the blue-eyed woman for long moments after she scurried past him on the trail. He had felt like a jerk when she had looked back and realized he was following her progress with his eyes. She had hastened her step and he felt like a proper prick for scaring her.

He was certain she was the woman from the grey house that he had camped behind a couple of nights before. From his tent that night, he could see her moving inside her house after darkness descended and she had turned on the interior lights. He had been too far away to see the details of her features but her long dark hair had mesmerized him, the way it tumbled down her back. Late in the evening she had gone to the upstairs deck and stood looking out over the moonlit ocean. Her small frame had been wrapped inside a dark sweater and he was pretty certain she had been crying. Her loneliness that night had been palpable and had made him feel lonely too, an emotion he didn't often experience despite being completely alone in the world.

She had looked more scared than sad today. He had seen her only a moment before she had noticed him on the trail. Her red knit hat had caught his eye. She had been walking toward him, lost in her thoughts, oblivious to him or anything else that might be lurking in the woods. He had wondered whether he should speak. Should he have done something to alert her to his presence? It had been too late to turn back on the trail and the trees were too dense to duck out of sight. He had felt a bit like a deer in the headlights waiting for impact. And then when she had finally noticed him she had looked terrified. He had wanted to reassure her but he couldn't find the words. He couldn't find his voice. Stupidly he had just stood there, staring at her.

She had stopped walking too and stared back at him. He had felt like they were playing some game of chicken. Who would move first? Who would break the stalemate? She had been the braver of the two of them. He had felt a moment of admiration at the nearly imperceptible straightening of her shoulders as she started slowly moving towards him. He respected her courage. Her beauty had astonished him.

John had been intoxicated by the scent of her as she cautiously walked past him. It reminded him of things he had long since forgotten; a hint of coconut and some fruity melon scent mixed with something more delicate and maybe floral. Even though the moment of their encounter was fleeting he had been bombarded with so many visceral impressions. Wide blue eyes, perhaps the biggest, bluest eyes he had ever seen, at least that he could remember. A single long dark braid of hair spilled from beneath her red hat, falling well past her shoulder. She was taller than he had expected, maybe 5'6" but she seemed thin, almost fragile. He hoped she wasn't sick. Her skin looked soft and he had a fleeting thought of running his fingers gently along her face. Her cheeks were flushed bright red, as were her full lips, maybe from the exertion of the hike, more likely from the shock of encountering him on her travels. He had felt desire surge through him, another relatively forgotten experience.

He could only imagine how he must look. He had little concern for vanity in his daily struggle to simply exist. He had let his hair and beard grow long out of necessity. The beard helped keep his face warm in winter and it was simpler to let his hair grow than have someone get close enough to cut it. He felt uncomfortable around people. They asked questions and he didn't have answers, at least none that he wanted to share. He attempted to trim both his beard and hair every few months with scissors, but admittedly it had been a while since he had bothered. It had been more than a month since he'd had a proper shower and it was getting too cold for sponge baths in the local ponds and rivers. So he probably didn't smell the greatest either.

He slumped to his knees, suddenly tired and weary of the life he was leading. He couldn't remember the last time he'd held a woman. Kissed her. Made love to her. Yet seeing the dark haired, blue-eyed woman today, having her scent tease his senses, having her pass by him so closely on the narrow forest trail that he could have reached out and touched her, he could imagine doing all those things. Touching her. Kissing her. Possessing her. His flesh stirred again. It happened so rarely that he welcomed the ache of arousal. He was grateful to feel something other than hopelessness, or worse, numbness.

He impatiently gave himself a mental shake and forced the implausible thoughts from his head, despite them being a welcomed reprieve from his harsh reality. He was cold and hungry and would sell one of his kidneys for a hot bath, decent meal and clean clothes. Such was the life of the transient, homeless man, the only life he knew. He had been roaming these woods for several days, staying on the periphery of the properties in the area, hoping to find an out-building that he could use for a while before he had to return to civilization. And inevitably people. He hadn't found anything though and the woman's reaction to him today was proof that it was time to move on, clean himself up, find work in the city south of here and let a room for the winter. At this rate he would be walking all day and well into the evening to reach St. John's and just his luck, it was starting to snow.

John pulled himself to his feet, adjusted the pack on his back and, with a wistful sigh over his shoulder, started walking. He had to forget the beautiful stranger, just as he had forgotten everything and everyone else in his life. He hadn't covered much ground when he heard a scream from the opposite direction. *Shit! It had to be the blue-eyed woman. What the hell had happened?* He turned and started retracing his path through the forest. She hadn't screamed when she stumbled across him watching her, so something a hell of a lot worse than him must have happened to her.

CHAPTER 3

Alyson cursed a litany of "fucks" as she lay writhing on the ground, grasping her injured ankle. She had been so eager to get back home that she had carelessly tripped on a fallen tree branch and found herself airborne at the edge of a small incline. Gravity won and she crashed to the ground, whacking her head off something hard and twisting her ankle. She hadn't heard anything snap in her foot so she was hopeful her ankle was sprained and not broken. Even so, it was hurting like a son of a bitch and she probably wouldn't be able to bear weight on it. She cursed her stupidity for walking so far from home with a storm approaching. She reached into her pocket and pulled out her phone, blinking back tears when she saw that the screen was smashed.

"No. No. No," she frantically muttered. She hoped it might still work but the cracked screen remained dark no matter how many times she pressed the power button. She couldn't even call for emergency assistance.

"Fuck!" she screamed in frustration. She was in serious trouble. People died in situations like this. What a fucking joke. On the day she resolved to become an active participant in her own life again, the universe decided to toy with her. She forced herself to take slow, deep breaths. Big mistake. Removing the focus from her throbbing ankle, shifted awareness to her aching head. She ran her fingers under her hat and they came away wet. Blood.

"Fuck! Fuck! Fuck!" she cried. The sight of blood made her weak. She closed her eyes and slowed her breathing, forcing herself to calm down. The coolness of the ground against her head actually helped the pain a little. She'd give herself a few moments to regain her equilibrium and then she'd find a stick she could use as a crutch to hobble her way out of these woods. The branch she had found earlier wasn't sturdy enough, plus she'd lost it in her tumble down the hill.

She couldn't help but notice that the snow was falling faster. At least the wind hadn't picked up yet, a small silver lining in this horrible mess. She looked around, taking care to move her head slowly to see if there was a tree branch or something she could use that would bear her weight. She carefully pushed herself into a sitting position, swallowing down the nausea that burned in her throat as the world tried to upright itself. Great, she probably had a concussion, too.

"Seriously?" she shouted, her voice quickly swallowed up by the trees towering all around her. She scooted a little to the left, ignoring the wet snow seeping through her jeans. She really had to get out of here. She was dressed for a hike on a mild autumn day, not for a late season blizzard. She reached above her head and grabbed onto a tree branch. She tried three times before successfully pulling herself upright. She leaned heavily against the tree, bearing all of her weight on her uninjured foot. The world was spinning and dizziness threatened her tenuous attempt to remain vertical. She rested her head against the tree and took several deep breaths before shifting some of her weight to her injured foot. She yelped as fiery pain shot through her foot and up her calf. Dammit! There was no way she was hiking out of here under her own steam.

But she simply could not stay in the woods. Staying here with a storm moving in meant certain death. No one knew she was here. No one would know she was missing. She tried crawling but the ground was so rugged that her injured foot was jostled by every tree root and rock. She rolled onto her back and took a few deep breaths. She tried moving backwards and it seemed to work better. It was slow going because she had to keep pausing to look behind her to make sure there were no rocks or branches that would cause further injury. The ground was uneven and the trail rough at best. Her back and arms were aching and her leg was tiring with the effort to lift her injured foot off the ground as much as possible as she dragged herself along. She had to stop every few minutes to keep the dizziness from overwhelming her. She was terrified of blacking out. The effort to move had her sweating profusely and the cold seeping in through her light layers of clothing chilled her to the core.

She had about three kilometers of ground to cover. She called out for help every few meters, just in case someone else was crazy enough to be out here hiking in the preface of the approaching storm. She thought of the stranger. There was no way he would hear her. They had been moving in opposite directions for more than twenty minutes. He was probably long gone. At this point, she wasn't sure if that was a hope or a fear.

To distract herself she thought of Joe as she painstakingly dragged herself through the forest. She let her thoughts drift back to the day they had met. It had been a rainy spring day and she had rushed to Vancouver General Hospital to check on her sister who had been admitted for an emergency appendectomy. She had been rummaging in her purse for change for the vending machine, completely oblivious to her surroundings, when she crashed into someone rounding a corner. That someone had been Joe, that is, Dr. Joseph Fisher. He had been in the final year of his residency at General. Alyson had gone sprawling to the floor and bumped her head.

Doctor Joe had been worried about a concussion so he insisted on examining her and running tests to ensure she was okay. She had thought he was the most handsome man she had ever seen. He had dark blond hair that was cut short and his eyes were deep blue and sparkled like he knew a secret. Like he knew *her* secrets. He had an easy smile and perfect white, straight teeth. She had been fixated on his mouth, watching it move as he spoke, as he smiled, as he contemplatively pressed his lips together while writing in her chart. She had wondered what it would be like to kiss his lips. To feel them on her mouth. Her body. He had actually made her swoon and it had nothing to do with the bump on her head. He was perfect, well except for an inch long scar that slashed through his left eyebrow. Otherwise, though, perfect.

He confirmed that she didn't have a concussion, but before Doctor Joe gave her the all clear, he wrote his name and number on a piece of paper and handed it to her with instructions to call him if she felt dizzy or nauseated. Then he asked her to go out with him. On a date. He admitted after the fact that it hadn't been particularly professional of him, but he risked it anyway. Turned out she made him swoon too. She accepted his dinner invitation and from that moment on they became inseparable, spending every available second together. She had never felt so completely at ease and so absolutely herself with anyone before. Joe had been created for her. She had been certain of that. They had only been dating six months when he asked her to move in with him. Two months later, on Christmas Eve, he proposed. They had enjoyed a whirlwind romance followed by a fairytale wedding next to a glacial lake in the mountains. They were supposed to have lived happily ever after. Together.

Alyson cried out in pain as a sharp rock dug into her backside. *Dammit to hell.* She had to be more careful. She had about all of the injuries she could handle at the moment. She still had so far to go and already her jeans and gloves were soaked through. She was cold and shivering and the dizziness was making her nauseated. She checked the gash on the back of her head. It was still bleeding. The snow was falling harder, the flakes bigger. She had only experienced a couple of early spring storms since moving here. One had been an outright blizzard that had been so much more dramatic than the modest snow falls in Vancouver. She had been warned that when a northeaster blew through, parts of the island would be shut down for hours, sometimes days. She had enjoyed the storms from the safety and comfort of her bed and breakfast, but out here in the middle of the action, not so much.

"You are not dying here today. You are not dying here today," she repeated the mantra to herself as she inched closer to home. She decided to try crawling again. Even though it was so much harder on her injured foot, she made faster time since she could see what was ahead of her. She crawled for as long as she could and when the pain became unbearable, she reverted to her backwards shuffle. Slowly but surely she made progress. Her fingers were so cold she couldn't even feel them and her legs and bum were growing numb too. *Damn that stranger!* If she hadn't encountered him she probably wouldn't have fallen. She'd be back home by now counting down the hours until five, when she could open up a bottle of merlot without too much guilt.

She thought of her gas fireplace in her beautiful living room and how desperately she wanted to be there right now. She imagined snuggling on the buttery soft leather couch in her flannel pajamas, with a fleece blanket draped around her shoulders and her hands wrapped around a mug of steaming coffee spiked with her favourite liqueur. She envisioned being toasty warm and dry and safe. She'd curl up on the couch and watch the snow as it piled higher and higher outside her window ledge. Maybe she'd close her eyes for a few moments and take a nap.

With a start she realized she had stopped moving and was falling asleep. It was probably her head, undoubtedly concussed. She was probably losing a lot of blood too, though she didn't want to think about that. She moved into the crawling position again and called for help. She was concerned by how weak her voice sounded. She tried yelling louder but she didn't have the strength to project her voice. Her foot was killing her and God knows how much more damage she was doing repeatedly bumping it like this but it was her best shot of getting to safety. She gritted her teeth against the pain and pressed on.

She remembered the first time she and Joe had made love. It had been their second date. He had invited her to his place and they had ordered Chinese food. Her fortune cookie had read, 'great adventures await you' and Joe had tacked on the phrase 'in bed', explaining it was something he and his friends always did in college to spice up the usually boring fortunes. They laughed and their eyes met and held. Alyson didn't even see Joe move. One moment he was seated on the floor across from her holding a cookie and the next she was flat on her back on the rug and he was kissing her, his body covering every inch of hers. They didn't even remove all of their clothing, only the bits and pieces necessary for him to drive inside of her, filling her body and her heart beyond full. She was certain that was the moment she fell in love with him. She had never had anyone look at her like that before, want her that desperately, that completely. That was the moment Dr. Joseph Fisher had ruined her for anyone else.

Hot tears ran down her cheeks as she tried to keep crawling forward. She was too numb. Too cold. Too exhausted. Too dizzy. The world was a twisting superlative of pain and nausea and it was swallowing her. She closed her eyes, telling herself it was just for a moment but deep inside she knew she was beat. With Joe's name on her lips, she gave herself over to the darkness and let the blissful oblivion of sleep claim her.

CHAPTER 4

John paused, certain he had heard her again but the only sound was the pounding of his own heartbeat and laboured breathing.

"Hello?" he called out as loudly as his seldom-used vocal chords would allow.

He listened intently but received no reply. The trails in the forest were not well-travelled paths and he was afraid that he was moving away from her. He kept pausing to listen, straining to hear something, anything, until his head hurt. Nothing.

He wondered if she had encountered a wild animal. He had seen moose in the forest but he didn't know if they would attack a human; maybe if they were cornered or threatened. He wondered if there were bears or wildcats. Coyotes. He was freaking himself out. Any of those animals could do serious damage to an unarmed person. He made himself move faster and kept yelling his hoarse hellos.

He was thankful that he hadn't started walking away after their encounter. If he had, he might not have heard her scream. She was still maybe fifteen minutes away from him though, perhaps more since he couldn't be certain which way she was moving through the forest and now the snow was obscuring everything. He wasn't even sure if this was the same path he had walked earlier that morning. The trees seemed denser than he remembered. He may have veered off the trail. He groaned in frustration. He had to find her and make sure she was okay. He called out into the trees again. Silence. Nothing but the sound of silence.

He remembered running through similar woods in northern Maine a couple of years back. Something had been chasing him then. A man. He had been squatting in what he thought was an abandoned cabin but it turned out it belonged to an ornery old bugger who didn't take kindly to a vagrant making himself at home. Luckily John was able to outrun the old coot. Forced out of the woods, he wandered into a small town on the coast. He had spent a couple of years there working as a deckhand on a fishing boat. It was the longest time he had spent in one place, at least that he could remember. The people there went about their own business and weren't interested in his. He had liked that. The pay on the fishing boat had been decent and for the first time in memory he had been earning more than he needed for basic survival. He saved every cent that he could, hiding his money in a couple of socks stuffed in a plastic bag at the bottom of his backpack. He had purchased his first luxury items in that little town; a small sketchpad, pencils and a used book. He loved reading and the used bookstore was a godsend, the matronly owner allowing him to exchange one book for another when he finished reading. The town didn't have a library so it had been an ideal arrangement and her kindness was one of the high points in his existence. The sketchbook and pencils were more perplexing to him. He hadn't ventured out that day with the intention of looking for those items, but when he saw them on display near the cash register of the shop, he knew instinctively that he should purchase them.

He remembered the first time he sat before a blank page with a sharpened pencil in hand. He had no idea what he would do with it but his hand seemed to move of its own volition. He was astonished to see the likeness of the fishing vessel he worked on, tied up at its berth in town. It wasn't just a passing resemblance, it was precise and detailed and recreated from memory. It brought him immeasurable joy to realize that he was gifted in some way. Perhaps his internal narrative was wrong. After years of listening to his mental voice whispering that he wasn't worthy of a home, a family or anything good, he was struck by the incomprehensible thought that perhaps he wasn't completely worthless after all. This font of creativity and beauty lived inside of him. That counted for something.

He sketched every night after that; drawings of the people he observed around the docks, the fish they caught, a puppy running along the rutted pavement, daisies growing wild on the grassy banks edging the shoreline. He filled every inch of the sketchpad and used his pencils until they were too stubby to sharpen with his pocketknife. He had to buy more. He could remember carefully counting out the precious dollars from his growing savings and walking into the store with a sense of excitement and anticipation. It was incredible having something to look forward to each day. It was a foreign feeling and he treasured the quiet hours he spent logging the details of his days through his art. He sometimes wondered where this hidden talent came from and how he might have used it had his life turned out differently. Had he not lost everything. Had he not been on the run for as long as he could remember.

He paused again, thinking he had heard something. He strained to listen, holding his breath, not moving a muscle. There! Yes! Definitely a cry for help. It sounded like it was coming from behind him though.

"Hello! I'm coming!" he yelled. Again he paused to listen but didn't hear a reply.

The voice had sounded like it was coming from south of him and to the right. He started moving in that direction. The trees were frustratingly dense so it was slow going. He picked his way carefully, stopping to listen now and then but he didn't hear her again.

"Hello! Hang in there! I'm coming!" he called again, cursing to himself as a jagged branch scratched his cheek.

He had to backtrack a couple of times to find space large enough for him to squeeze through in the thick undergrowth. He always carried a small axe strapped to his pack but the strap had broken at some point the day before and the axe had fallen off without him realizing it. He hadn't missed it until last night when he reached for it to cut branches for a fire. He sure as hell could use it right now. His gloves were already shredded from trying to break away boughs that slowed his progress. Finally he emerged in a small clearing that seemed to form part of the slightly more defined trail that he had walked earlier in the day. But was she north or south of him now? He called out again but there was no reply. The snow seemed to be coming down even faster. He hoped it wasn't a big storm. There were still several hours of daylight left but, depending on the amount of trouble she was in when he found her, he might not have sufficient time to get them out of the forest before nightfall. The sun set early this far north in late autumn. He could probably set up the tent but that wasn't ideal either, especially if the snow didn't stop soon.

He glanced down and noticed the snow next to his foot was tinged pink. *Blood.* She was bleeding. At least he knew he was on the right trail. He started walking south and after a few feet he saw another smudge of pink in the snow, this one a little fresher. He walked as quickly as he dared on the wet snow covered path that was getting slicker with every snowflake that fell. He peered around every bend expectantly, swallowing his disappointment each time she failed to appear in his line of sight. He was giving up hope when he finally glimpsed the bright red of her hat a few feet ahead. His knees went weak with relief and he had to swallow back an unexpected rush of emotion. He started to run when he realized she wasn't moving.

He knelt in the snow next to her, shrugging out of his pack and quickly glancing over her to check for possible injuries. The knees of her jeans looked bloodied but she didn't appear to have been mauled by a wild animal so most likely she had fallen and hurt herself. Her eyes were closed. He removed his glove and gingerly pressed his finger against the carotid artery in her neck. There was a pulse, thank God. He gently shook her but she didn't respond.

"Wake up. Come on lady. Wake up now. Please. Can you hear me?" His voice was gritty and desperate.

He shook her harder and her eyes fluttered open. She recoiled in fear when she saw him.

"It's okay," he reassured her. "I won't hurt you. What happened? Are you injured?"

She shook her head but even that slight motion caused her to grimace in pain. She looked at him as though she was fighting the internal battle of a lifetime. He could only imagine what she was thinking, *trust the bum or die in the woods.*

"Jesus lady. I won't hurt you but there's no way in hell I'm leaving you here alone in the cold."

"Maybe you could call for help," she whispered.

"I don't have a phone. Do you?"

"It's broken," her voice broke on the words as she fought tears.

"Well then, like it or not, I am the help. Now let's try this again. Where are you injured?" he asked forcing his voice to stay calm despite the panic rising inside of him.

She continued to look at him warily as she spoke, "I tripped and fell down a hill. My right foot is sprained or broken. Back of my head is bleeding. I feel dizzy and cold." Her voice was growing weaker and her eyes were fluttering shut again.

"Hey, lady. You have to stay awake. You can't sleep right now. Do you understand?"

"Yes. Concussion. I know."

"Good. So stay with me. Keep your eyes open for me."

"Okay. I'll try."

"What's your name?"

"Alyson."

"Hi Alyson. I'm John. I am going to help you get out of here. Okay?"

"Okay," she whispered, her voice barely audible, as though that was all of the energy she could muster.

"Can I take a quick look at your head?" John asked.

"It hurts," she said, but nodded her permission.

"I'm going to remove your hat. Okay?"

Again she nodded.

John carefully pulled off her hat and gave it to her to hold. She clumsily tried to push her frozen hands inside of the warm wool. John noticed what she was doing and helped her, tugging the hat firmly around her hands.

"Better?" he asked.

She smiled and nodded.

John was jolted by her smile. She was so beautiful it pained him deep inside just to look at her, as though he couldn't process all of her at once. It was an odd and unfamiliar feeling.

"I'm going to help you sit so I can see the back of your head. Okay?"

"I get dizzy and sick," she warned him.

"We'll go slow," he said, his voice gruff.

Staying true to his word, he slowly helped her sit, stopping every few seconds to help her adjust to the change in her positioning.

"Doing okay?" he asked.

She nodded and attempted another smile but it came off as more of a grimace. She was obviously in a world of pain.

He slowly moved so he was kneeling behind her. She was sitting with her weight leaned slightly forward, her hands inside the hat resting on her lap. He gently parted her hair to see the gash on the back of her head. It was still bleeding a little but seemed to be clotting and would probably be okay until he could get her back to her house. Hopefully someone was there waiting for her. She needed to get to a hospital.

"The bleeding has almost stopped. I'm going to pull up your hood to keep your head warm. Is that okay?"

"Yes. Thank you," she replied. "My hands are starting to tingle inside the hat so I don't want to give it up."

"You don't have to. Keep your hands inside. What about your ankle? I could try to splint it."

"Even with a splint I don't think I could bear weight on it," her voice hitched on a sob as she blinked back tears.

"Hey. It's okay. I'll carry you. If that's okay?" he offered.

"Thank you," she smiled. "I don't think there's any other choice."

"It's going to be slow going. The ground is really slick and I don't want to risk falling with you and hurting you even more."

"You'll be faster than my pathetic attempts to crawl out of here. Really. Thank you." Her big blue eyes were brimming with tears. John felt something twist in his heart. He had to get her back to safety. She was shivering and her voice was weak. He needed to get her dry and warm as soon as possible.

"I have a sleeping bag in my pack. I want to wrap you in it to keep you warm. Okay?"

She nodded as her tears spilled over.

The sleeping bag was in the top of his pack. He quickly unrolled and unzipped it on the ground next to Alyson.

"I'm going to lift you onto the bag. Okay?"

She nodded.

John hesitated for a moment. This was the most contact he had had with another person in as long as he could remember. He gently placed one arm under her lower back and the other under her knees and lifted her off the wet ground. She weighed next to nothing. She was even smaller than he first thought. He placed her on the opened sleeping bag and quickly zipped it up around her. He also tied her hood tightly under her chin. She burrowed her face into the sleeping bag.

God she smelled so good. The fear was gone from her eyes. There was still wariness but mostly he could see relief.

"Okay, Alyson. Just rest there for a moment and try to get warm. I really think I should splint your foot, just to keep it stable. I'm going to look for a small branch. Okay?"

She nodded, just her big blue eyes visible from inside of the bag.

"Don't go to sleep."

"I won't."

He went to the closest tree and, using a small knife he pulled from his pocket, laboriously cut through a medium sized branch, quickly stripping off the small twigs along its length. He rummaged around in his pack and took out a fleece sweater, wrapping it around the branch to provide some cushioning against her leg.

"I'm going to unzip the bag for just a moment to get the splint in place. Okay?"

"Yes. Of course. Thank you."

His eyes met hers for a moment and then darted away. He secured the makeshift splint with two of his t-shirts and zipped the bag up again.

"Hopefully that will help stabilize your ankle and ease the pain a little while we hike out of here."

"It already hurts less and I think the cold probably helped ease the swelling as well."

"I'm going to get back into my pack and I'm going to get you out of here. Sound good?"

"Leave the pack. It will slow us down. I'll replace everything."

"Everything I own is in this pack. It won't slow me down I promise. It's like part of me and I can't leave it behind. You good with that?"

"Sorry. Yes. Of course. My house is south of here, about two and a half kilometers," she said, as John lifted her effortlessly off the ground.

"It's okay. I know where you live." The instant the words fell from his lips he regretted them. Her eyes widened in alarm and she looked every bit as frightened as she had when she first saw him.

CHAPTER 5

"How do you know where I live?" she asked, her voice quivering, betraying the depth of her unease. She almost demanded that he put her down but really, what the hell good would that do.

"I camped in the woods behind your house a couple of nights ago. I saw you on your deck. I wasn't spying or anything. I just happened to see you."

"Why were you camping in my woods this time of year?"

"Long story. Let's focus on getting you back to your house. We have more than a mile to cover at least and I really need to focus on every step. Okay?"

"You said mile not kilometer. Are you American?"

"I don't know."

"You don't know? What do you mean you don't know?"

"Like I said, long story. For now though I want to get you out of this snow. Okay?"

"Okay. There's a bad storm moving in."

"Great," he muttered.

Alyson had no idea what to make of this man. Part of him scared her out of her wits. He had camped in her woods? He knew where she lived? Had he been stalking her? Or was it simply a coincidence? Yet he was being so gentle with her and attentive to her injuries and comfort. She could remember reading somewhere that sociopaths were apathetic, so these weren't the actions of a serial killer. Were they?

She had been startled to see him when he shook her awake a few minutes ago. However, she quickly realized he was her only chance of getting out of here before the storm worsened. She honestly had thought she would die in the woods and was still silently censuring herself for getting caught in such a dangerous situation. She thought of her parents and Syd and how devastated they would have been if she had gone missing. She had put her family through enough in the past two years since Joe's death. She felt a pang of regret for how withdrawn she had become. Their concern stemmed from love and genuine desire for her happiness and she had repeatedly pushed them away. She owed them all apologies. Lois, too.

She stole a quick glance at her rescuer. John. Did he really not know if he was American? How was that possible? She would insist that he tell her everything when they made it back to her house. Funny but she barely noticed the stale smell of his clothing now. His sleeping bag was keeping her warm despite the wet jeans and jacket she was wearing. It was helping to trap her body heat and her hands were still snug inside of her hat. The pins and needles in her fingers were finally subsiding. She was also touched by the way he had wrapped the tree branch in his sweater to make it more comfortable for her. His kindness and thoughtfulness reminded her of things Joe might do.

His eyes were green. A startling jade against his wind weathered face. She estimated him to be in his late 30s or early 40s, just a handful of years older than her most likely. He was cautiously picking each step as he moved them through the forest. He glanced at her and caught her watching him. She felt his body tense in response and he quickly looked away. He seemed uncomfortable with eye contact. She wondered why.

She also wondered why his voice was so raspy but she couldn't summon the energy to ask.

Alyson closed her eyes, just for a moment. Her head was throbbing and she desperately wanted to sleep. It felt good to drift off. She was so tired. It was overwhelming. She could hear someone saying her name but she ignored it. Nothing was more important right now than resting. She felt as though she was being shaken and the voice saying her name was getting louder and angrier. *What the hell?*

Alyson woke with a jolt. John had stopped walking and he was indeed shaking her and calling her name.

"Oh thank God," he said, relief evident in his voice. "You wouldn't wake up. I couldn't get you to wake up."

"Sorry. I felt so tired. Just wanted to rest for a moment."

"You can't sleep. If you have a concussion you have to stay awake for something like twenty-four hours."

"I don't think I can do it."

"You have to."

"Okay. Sorry. I'll try harder."

"I'm going to set you down for a moment. I need a second. Okay?"

"Of course."

John carefully set her down so that her back was leaning against a tree and he walked away from her.

"You're not going to leave me here, are you?"

"What? Of course not," he whipped around to face her. "I just need a moment."

He ventured further away and she realized, belatedly, he probably needed to urinate or something. She could actually stand to go herself though it was impossible given she was trussed up in the stranger's sleeping bag. She definitely didn't want to ask him for help with that!

He returned a few moments later, but still avoided her eyes. She was itching to ask him more about his story but he had made it clear that he didn't want to talk about it. She wondered what would happen when they finally reached her place. He couldn't camp outside in the storm. And he was actively saving her life. The noble and gracious thing to do would be to offer him shelter until the storm passed. Would she truly be safe with him in her home though? Huh, did she really have a choice?

"You're getting pretty wet," she commented, taking in his snow covered hat and jacket.

"It's okay. We should make it back to your place in less than an hour."

"I wish we could magic ourselves there right now," she mused.

He smiled at the frivolity of her words. She couldn't help notice that when he smiled he looked a decade younger and not nearly as scary looking.

"Let's hit the trail again. You ready?"

"Yes. Sorry you have to do all of the heavy lifting."

"You're pretty light, lucky for me."

Again that grin and the hint of a sense of humour. She was becoming increasingly curious about his story. She had a feeling there was much more to this man than she first thought. Her mother had told her she needed to go on an adventure during a recent phone call. Alyson wondered if this qualified.

He picked her up opposite to the way he held her last time.

"Are you comfortable?" he asked.

"I am, thank you," she smiled.

He quickly looked away and his cheeks turned red.

"Your face is bleeding," Alyson said, pulling her hand out of the warmth of the sleeping bag and tracing her gloved finger against his cheek.

John stopped walking and stared at her. He looked as though she had burned his flesh with her touch.

"Sorry," she said. "Does it hurt?"

"No. Just not used to being touched."

"Oh." Alyson wasn't sure what else to say to that as she stuffed her hands back into the sleeping bag. Another question to add to the growing list she'd bombard him with later.

They walked in silence for several minutes. The snow was transforming the forest into a fairytale setting. The branches were already laden with snow and the trees looked pretty. Magical. Alyson thought about the upcoming Christmas season. She had always enjoyed Christmas but since losing Joe she hadn't celebrated, choosing instead to hibernate through the entire holiday. Last year she had spent Christmas day with her parents and Sydney but returned to her lonely condo by late afternoon. That had been as much seasonal cheer as she could muster. Maybe this year she'd make an attempt to celebrate again. She'd think about getting a tree for her new home. Her living room had a wall of floor to ceiling windows that overlooked the ocean. A tree would look perfect against that backdrop.

She stole another glance at John, wondering if he celebrated Christmas. She was willing to bet the bank that it was just another day for him. She wondered if he had family. A wife. Children. If so, had they left him or had he left them? How does one end up with everything he owns in a pack on his back? So many damn questions.

A gust of wind suddenly whipped around them, blowing snow off the branches overhead and blanketing them.

"Oh no. That's not good, is it?" Alyson asked.

"Nope. Not good at all," he replied, shaking the excess snow off them as best he could without stopping.

"Every step brings us closer to my place. Let's focus on that."

"Good plan," he replied. He glanced at her, seemed about to say something but remained silent.

"What?" she asked.

"It's nothing," he gruffly answered.

"Tell me. Please."

"Well I was wondering if perhaps I might be able to wait out the storm in your garage. If the winds continue gusting they are going to make tenting next to impossible."

"You absolutely cannot stay in my garage," she answered incredulously.

"Sorry," he spared her a tentative glance but immediately looked away, as was becoming his custom.

"You'll stay in the house. I have two guest rooms."

"I cannot stay in your house. I don't want to put you out in any way," he firmly objected.

"John! You're literally saving my life this very moment. I insist that you stay at the house until the storm passes. It's the least I can do and I won't take no for an answer."

He looked as though he wanted to argue further but instead quietly said, "Thank you."

His voice was gruff but she liked that his mouth curled up into the ghost of a smile again. She definitely had ambiguous thoughts about her unexpected houseguest. His actions didn't seem like those of someone intending to do harm. She was probably being too naive and trusting but what choice did she really have in this impossible situation. He was helping her and she would help him in return. Besides, it might be nice to not be alone in the storm. The power would undoubtedly go out. She had been warned it usually did with heavy snows and high winds though she had not personally experienced that yet. She hoped they were hours away from that though. On the heels of that thought another gust of wind pummeled them, stealing her breath. Alyson buried her face in John's shoulder and offered another prayer of thanks that she was not still alone in the woods, slowly freezing to death in the storm.

CHAPTER 6

John stopped as another gust of wind swooped down around them. It was brutal with its icy North Atlantic bite, making it nearly impossible to breathe or walk in the driving snow. He hoped the gusts were well spaced so they could make better time. By his estimation they had less than thirty minutes of hiking left.

"Is there some landmark in the woods near your house so we'll know we haven't walked too far?" he asked.

"Yes. I tied bright orange nylon ribbon on a couple of the trees when I first moved here. I was afraid I'd get lost when I started hiking in this area. They're at about eye level for me."

"That was smart thinking. The snow is making everything look the same so the ribbons will help."

She smiled at him and his insides quivered. He wondered if he'd have this reaction to any woman in these circumstances, simply because it had been so long since he'd been this close to another person, let alone a beautiful, vulnerable one such as Alyson. Or was it her? Was there something about her specifically? In any case, she made him uncomfortable and itchy and hard. They walked in silence for several minutes, the wind making it increasingly difficult to talk. He was relieved that she seemed more alert and her voice was stronger. That had to be a good sign.

"Are you still warm in there?" he asked.

"Much warmer than you are, I imagine," she replied.

"We should be at your place soon. I'd estimate another twenty min..." The wind stole his breath and his last words. Alyson had ducked her head against his shoulder again and he had no choice but to stop walking and turn his face into the top of her hood-covered head, just to catch his breath. The gusts were coming faster and lasting longer and they were bloody frigid.

"I've heard of people perishing in storms like this just meters from their homes. They get disoriented in the whiteouts," she said, clearly scared for their safety.

"That is not going to happen to us! We have your orange ribbons to guide us. Your house is no distance from the tree line. We find the ribbons, we're as good as saved. Okay?"

"Okay," she smiled. Jesus, that smile was going to be the death of him.

He walked as quickly as he dared in the blinding snow, scanning the trees for any sign of the orange ribbons. The next gust of wind was startling in its intensity. It almost knocked him over. He widened his stance and burrowed his face against Alyson. Her hood had slipped a little and he belatedly realized his mouth was pressed against the bare skin of her temple. Amazingly, despite the harrowing conditions they were in, all of the blood in his body rushed to his groin. How on earth was it possible to have an erection *now*? He was grateful she was oblivious to the reawakening of his libido. He had to find a way to rein it in. God! Of all things!

"That was a bad one," the panic in her voice evident.

"Yeah. It's probably going to get a lot worse though but we'll be safe long before then."

He hoped he sounded confident. Truth was, he was scared shitless. People did die in situations like this. Where the fuck was the orange ribbon? He was pretty certain they were still on the trail so that was a positive at least. Despite Alyson weighing next to nothing, he was tiring. His arms were aching and his legs were threatening to cramp from the tension in his body as he cautiously executed each step. He knew he should try to stretch his leg muscles to keep them from going into spasms but he didn't want to lose the valuable minutes that would take. The next gust did take him off his feet. Luckily he fell backwards into a heap of snow-laden branches, breaking their fall.

"Shit. Are you okay?" he asked.

"Yes. Are you? That was a hard fall."

"It really wasn't that bad. I'm good. I'm going to tuck you under this big branch for just a minute. You should be sheltered in there. I was putting this off but I really need to stretch. Leg cramps."

"Of course."

There was no longer a choice; he had to take a couple of minutes. He rationalized that it wouldn't do either of them any good if his legs went into spasms and he couldn't walk. He braced himself against a sturdy tree and flexed each leg in turn at the ankle, extending the muscles and then relaxing. It was painful but hopefully it would get him through the next few minutes. So damn close to safety! He focused his thoughts on the welcoming warmth of Alyson's house. That was such a sweet incentive to keep moving and push past this latest obstacle. He could tell that she was shivering again. The snow was seeping through the sleeping bag. His own feet felt like clumsy blocks of ice. Every step was getting increasingly painful. And fuck! That wind! It was brutal. He had experienced bad storms in Maine but he had a feeling this one might outrank them all.

"I think that helped," he said, his mouth curving upward in a tentative smile. He wasn't used to smiling. Or talking.

"Good," she replied. "Home stretch now." Her eyes were looking heavy again.

He lifted her back into his arms, ignoring his screaming, aching muscles. He would get her home if it was the last thing he did.

"I have several pre-made meals in my freezer," she said, whether to distract her or him, he wasn't sure.

"Oh yeah?"

"Yes. I've discovered a wonderful deli in downtown St. John's. I buy two of everything every couple of months. I hate cooking for just myself. This is easier. What would you like when we get home? Meatloaf? Soup? Shepherd's pie? Lasagna?"

His answer was waylaid by another strong gust of wind. He was ready this time though and stood strong against it. They burrowed into each other and John couldn't help but be a little selfishly thankful for the storm. He might not experience intimacy like this again for decades. He was a little unnerved by how much he liked it. Being close to Alyson wasn't freaking him out like human contact usually did. He'd wonder why that was later when he had the luxury to ponder such things. For now he drank in her warmth and scent and waited for the wind to abate enough to cover another few feet of ground.

"Where are those fucking ribbons?" Alyson asked.

John laughed, the sound foreign but welcomed. She looked at him questioningly.

"I wondered the same thing, verbatim, just a few minutes ago. We have to be almost there." He couldn't remember the last time he had laughed. How odd to have forgotten the sound of your own laughter.

"I think more than twenty minutes have passed."

"Probably, but that's okay. We're still moving forward. We're okay."

Alyson nodded and tucked her face into his shoulder. God he hoped he didn't smell too awful. He knew under less extenuating circumstances there was no way someone like

Alyson would voluntarily want to spend time with someone like him. That realization sparked something inside of him. He felt an overwhelming urge to try to be better for her or for him. Maybe both. Of all the days he'd spent on the run, no one day had impacted him quite like this one. He supposed that was to be expected when their lives hung in the balance of him getting them to safety.

"Is there a closer house? A neighbour?" he asked.

"The houses are at least a kilometer apart in this area and mine is the last one in this direction. My place is closest."

"We'll get there. Don't worry. I promise I will get you home safely," he assured her.

He squinted into the snow, straining to see the orange ribbon, praying to a God he had long forgotten existed. He just wanted to get Alyson home.

CHAPTER 7

Alyson had never experienced cold like this. While the sleeping bag had really helped at first, now it was soaking wet and that wetness was seeping into the marrow of her bones. She dreaded the wind gusts. They were so violent and vicious and they scared the hell out of her. She kept swallowing back her panic, every breath a conscious effort to remain calm. John was doing his very best and she was grateful to him. The trail was rugged and twisted and hilly; it was challenging under the best of circumstances. There was no doubt in her mind that she owed him her life. Tears threatened as she thought about what would have happened to her if he hadn't come along. She fought those, too. She would be as strong as him. She owed him that.

"I see the ribbons!" he yelled. "I see them!"

She raised her head to peek into the storm and the frigid gale took her breath. She quickly tucked her head back into his shoulder. How the hell could he even breathe and keep moving in these icy blasts? The sustained winds were as bad as the earlier gusts, the trees offering minimal protection against the onslaught of the storm.

She lifted her face enough to shout against his ear, "The path veers left here. Follow it and we'll come out in my yard. We're just a couple hundred meters from my house. You did it! Thank God you did it!"

"Don't jinx it! Let's save the thanks until we're actually inside your house. Anything in your yard I can look for to help guide us to the house?"

"There's a huge blue spruce and a maple tree. We should come out between those."

They kept edging forward and after a couple of minutes John said, "I see the maple but no blue spruce."

"We're probably too far to the left. Go right a little. The house should be visible any moment."

The winds were relentless in the open expanse of the backyard. It was nearly impossible to see anything. Alyson couldn't lift her face for any more than a couple of seconds. She marveled yet again that John was still somehow moving and breathing.

"Oh thank Christ. I see it!" he said. His voice broke with emotion or maybe it was the thievery of the wind.

"Go straight to the back door. I have the key in my pocket." Alyson started rummaging around in the tight confines of the sleeping bag. Her jacket was wet and her hands were so cold that it took several attempts before she was able to successfully unzip her jacket pocket to retrieve the keys. There was a small porch leading to the back door but it did little to block the wind. John angled her best he could so she could unlock the door but her hands were too cold and she dropped the key ring. By the grace of God the keys didn't fall between the floorboards of the back porch.

"I'm going to have to set you down for a second so I can pick up the keys and unlock the door."

"Yes. Yes. Do it!"

Alyson tried to burrow her face into the sleeping bag but it had slipped. The wind and snow left her gasping for her breath. She had never experienced anything like this and she hoped to hell she never did again. John's hands were probably more numbed than hers and he was struggling to get the key into the lock and turn it. Finally the definitive snap of the lock opening reached their ears and the door swung inward, a warm welcome and a safe haven from this godforsaken storm.

John quickly scooped Alyson up and brought her into the house, kicking the door shut behind them. He gently set her down on the bench that ran along the short wall of the mudroom and unzipped the sleeping bag, letting it pool around her hips. The tears that she had been holding back for the last hour or more started to fall. She couldn't stop. Sobs wracked her body and she howled. John stood in front of her, looking terrified and uncertain. His beard and eyebrows and even his eyelashes were crusted with snow. That just made her cry harder. She'd be dead if it wasn't for him. *She'd be dead. If it wasn't for him.* That truth kept playing over and over in her mind.

Alyson tried to apologize but all she could manage were hiccoughs and hitched breaths. She was shaking uncontrollably, partly from the emotion but mostly from being so overwhelmingly cold.

"Thank you," she cried. "Thank you for coming back for me. For saving me."

"It's okay," he said, in his deep, gruff voice. "You're safe. It's okay." He sat next to her and clumsily wrapped his arm around her. She hesitated for a moment and then accepted his comfort, winding her arm around his broad chest in an awkward hug. Surprisingly the sound of his voice and his stilted attempts to console her actually calmed her down. She took several deep breaths and wiped her runny nose with the sleeve of her jacket.

"I'm sorry," she finally managed to gulp out between her abating sobs.

"It's okay. You've had a helluva day. Are you okay now?"

"Yes," she smiled.

"Good. We really need to get out of these wet clothes. We have to get warm."

"I know. Let's take off what we can here."

He supported her weight and tugged the sleeping bag from under her and dumped it on the large rug that covered most of the ceramic tiled floor in the generously sized mudroom. Then he unzipped her sodden jacket, his fingers inadvertently brushed against her breasts and his gaze bumped into hers.

"Sorry," he muttered.

"It's okay," she replied. "I'll work on getting the splint off. You get out of your jacket and boots." Now if only her numb fingers would cooperate.

John was having equal difficulty but finally he shrugged out of his coat, taking care to hang it on one of the hooks in the mudroom. He reached for hers and did the same. His boots proved more frustrating, his hands clumsily trying to untie the knots and failing.

"Can you pull them off?" she asked.

"No. Not without untying the bloody laces. I always knot them when I'm hiking so they don't come untied."

"Cut the laces. We can replace them. There are scissors in the kitchen through the doorway on the left."

"I have my knife." He pulled it from his pocket and after two attempts, successfully opened it and sliced through the laces on both boots. He sat on the bench next to Alyson and tugged them off.

"Christ the pins and needles are the worst," he swore.

"I have that joy to look forward to," she smirked.

"Are you doing okay?" he asked.

"I get dizzy when I hold my head down."

"I'll help you," he offered when he noticed she had only managed to untie one of the two t-shirts holding the splint in place. He knelt on the floor in front of her and untied the second t-shirt. He pulled off her left boot and she gasped as those same pins and needles attacked her foot.

"Damn, that hurts," she mumbled.

"I'll be as gentle as I can with your injured foot but it's probably going to get wrenched. The boots are a snug fit and you don't have laces we can cut or even zippers."

"I know. Please get it off me."

"Okay. Ready?"

She nodded and gritted her teeth. He pulled as gently as he could but she still gasped as her foot was freed from the boot. It hurt so much she felt like she might get sick.

"Deep breaths. That's the worst now."

She nodded and gave him a small smile.

"Take off the socks, too, please."

He pulled off her socks and then his own.

"The bathroom in the downstairs guest room has a built in seat so if you could help me into that one I'll manage to undress myself and have a hot shower. You can use the main bathroom upstairs. There are guest robes on the back of the bathroom door. Please help yourself. Okay?"

"Alyson I cannot tell you how much I'm looking forward to this shower. Just to feel clean and warm. That is truly a gift. Thank you."

"I'm the one who owes you my gratitude. You saved my life."

"I did what anyone would do."

She wondered if anyone else would have risked their own life the way he had risked his. It was an added reassurance that he was a good and decent person. He lifted her into his arms and she gave him directions through the lower floor of the house to the guest suite. At her request he set her down on the built-in bench that ran along two sides of the custom glass block enclosed shower. He placed the towels and robe she requested on the edge of the counter next to the shower door. He insisted on checking her head again.

"The bleeding has stopped and it doesn't look as bad as I feared." The relief in his voice was unmistakable.

"Good," she smiled, shivering in her wet clothes.

"What about your knees? They're bleeding too."

"They're just banged up from crawling. Nothing serious."

"Are you sure you're going to be okay?" he asked.

"Yes. I'll keep my head upright as much as possible. I can move along the seat and the shower controls are low enough to reach. I'll be fine. The main bathroom is the first door on your right at the top of the stairs. Go warm up."

"Thanks, I will," he turned to leave.

"John?"

He turned at the door, "Yes?"

"I almost forgot. There are soaps, shampoos and other toiletries in the cabinet under the sink over there. It's the middle door I think. They're not all girly," she smiled, "I keep a few manly things on hand for when my dad visits. No worries, you won't end up smelling like me."

"That wouldn't be the worst thing in the world," he smiled. He had such a striking smile. This one actually reached his eyes and completely transformed him. Very nice. She admonished herself for thinking he was scary earlier. After the hell they just endured, he was a veritable superhero. And he had better not do anything to alter that opinion. God she hoped she was doing the right thing.

He opened the cupboard door and found the items she had mentioned as well as a plastic sealed deodorant.

"There are unopened toothbrushes in the bottom drawer in the upstairs bathroom. You'll also find antiseptic cream in one of the cabinets that you can use on your cheek. Rummage around and please use whatever you need."

"Thank you, Alyson. Please be careful in the shower," he said as he left the bathroom, closing the door behind him. She sat perfectly still, listening as he closed the guest bedroom door as well. She waited until she heard his footsteps upstairs and then started wiggling out of her wet clothes. They were plastered to her skin and her fingers still felt frozen and clumsy so it was a bit of a struggle. Her knees were bruised and had several scratches but only a couple looked like they had been bleeding. Her bottom was sore too and was probably bruised. She scooted along the bench until she could reach the shower controls. The warm water felt heavenly and she carefully inched back so she was directly under the spray. The tears came again. There were moments on the trail that she honestly didn't think they'd make it back. Her limbs felt heavy and her movements sluggish as her body warmed up but she didn't care. She'd take whatever residual aches and pains came her way. Happily. They were alive and safe from the storm. Thanks to John.

CHAPTER 8

John stood under the shower spray and let the hot water touch every inch of him. God that felt so good. It had been too long since he had experienced the comfort of a hot shower. His recent wilderness sponge baths had been less than ideal and not overly effective. But this was paradise. The shampoo and body wash had a subtle woodsy scent that he liked. He thought about Alyson's scent and he instantly hardened. Again. Christ what was he going to do about this? Maybe if he relieved himself, his libido would settle down. Hesitantly, he wrapped his soapy fist around his throbbing length and closed his eyes. He braced his free hand against the tiled wall and allowed himself to bask in the memory of how her temple had felt against his lips. That's all it took. In less than two minutes he was panting like a teenage boy, streams of ejaculate spraying hard against the shower wall. It had been years since he had felt the need for sexual release. He often had the notion that he could have been a priest. But this woman was awakening a lust so deep and primal within him that it scared the shit out of him. He sensed it would scare her too. He forced himself to think of more pedestrian things, cleaned his splattered offerings from the tiles and reluctantly turned off the hot water.

He dried off and slipped a dark blue flannel robe over his clean body. God this felt so damn good. He had never known such luxury and he envied people who lived like this. Though he supposed most people did. He was often the exception to the proverbial rules. He found a new toothbrush in the drawer she had mentioned and spent long minutes brushing his teeth. His own toothbrush was downstairs in his pack and it was worn.

He felt so clean and refreshed that he didn't want to put on his dirty, threadbare clothes again. The robe provided enough coverage that Alyson shouldn't be offended if he left it on. He gathered up his wet clothes from the bathroom floor and when he stepped into the upstairs hallway he could hear the water running in the guest bath downstairs. He hoped she was okay. He glanced into the open doors off the landing on the second floor. The room next to the bathroom was her office. There was a large glass and steel desk set up against the wall beneath the only window in the room. He wondered what type of job she had or if she worked at all. She seemed pretty well off. Her house was spectacular, at least what he had seen so far. He couldn't imagine living in a space like this. A second door revealed a bedroom, which appeared to be another guest room, presumably the room she had offered him in the forest. He wouldn't hold her to that, though. The garage was fine for him. The third door on the landing led to what he assumed was Alyson's bedroom. He could see the glass slider that led to the second story deck. Her room was decorated in shades of pale blues and greens. Not what he expected. Her bed was huge and looked incredibly inviting. His mind went there, he couldn't help himself. He imagined them in that bed together. Kissing. Loving. It was a nice thought but an impossible dream. He had learned a long time ago not to dream. Not to dare. His dreams didn't come true. Ever.

Another thought slammed into him. Hard. What if there was a husband? Obviously no one else was here now but maybe she had a significant other who was away on business or something. What if Alyson already belonged to someone else? The thought bothered him more than he wanted to admit. And the fact that he felt bothered at all pissed him off. What the fuck was wrong with him? What difference would it make if she were happily married? He would be on his way again in a day or two.

He hastily turned and hurried down the stairs, dumping his wet clothes in the mudroom. There were two doors on the wall to his right; one led to the garage and the second to a spacious laundry room with the flashiest washer and dryer he had ever seen. He'd never figure out how to operate those. He walked back through the kitchen, taking in the details he had missed the first time through. He was amazed by the shiny expanses of granite counter tops, double ovens and a gas cook top. The cabinets were a sage green colour with etched glass fronts that distorted the appearance of the contents behind them. The dark mahogany island was massive with four bar stools neatly stored beneath the granite overhang. The light fixture over the island was incredible. He had never seen anything like it; twisted metal holding six suspended etched glass cylinders. It looked custom made and more like cutting edge art than a practical light shade.

He wandered back to the first floor guest room, passing a living room with soaring ceilings, a large grey brick fireplace and a wall of tall windows that he assumed overlooked the ocean. Right now they were framing the whiteout that was raging outside. He shivered in relief that they were no longer outside in that hellish storm. The winds were howling and relentless. He tapped lightly on the guest room door but didn't hear a reply. He pushed the door open slightly speaking her name. No answer. She must still be in the bathroom. He momentarily debated whether he should simply wait or knock to let her know he was there. He decided to knock.

"Alyson. Are you okay? Can I help you to the living room or something?"

"Yes please. It's okay to come in."

He opened the door and she was leaning against the double-sink vanity. The sinks were those fancy type that looked like glass bowls sitting on the counter top. He liked them.

"You're standing," he said, surprised.

"Sort of. I can't bear weight on my right foot but I managed to drag myself around the room, holding on to the counter. I really needed to use the facilities," she blushed.

"Feeling warmer?"

"Actually I'm chilled again. Would you please help me to the living room? There's a gas fireplace and it will help warm us."

"Of course," he said, approaching her.

"I think I can walk if you let me lean on you," she suggested.

He moved next to her, and placed his arm around her on her injured side. She tried to hobble but the moment she placed pressure on her injured foot, it went weak and she gasped in pain.

"This is silly," he muttered, sweeping her up into his arms.

Alyson gave a small cry of surprise and her arms instinctively wrapped around his neck. He stood frozen in place and she followed his gaze. The front of her robe had gaped open, revealing the swell of her left breast and the very edge of her areola.

"You best cover that up," he demanded, his voice deep and rough.

Alyson hastily pulled her robe together, keeping her hand fisted on the material to ensure it didn't slip open again. John silently cursed the erection that raged uncontained beneath his robe. How on earth was he going to survive this woman? Goddammit!

He quickly moved to the living room and gently set her down on one of the two cream coloured leather couches that sat opposite each other with a large wooden coffee table between them. The leather was incredibly soft. She was still clutching her robe. He noticed a blanket tossed over the edge of the second couch and retrieved it, unfolded it and placed it over her.

"Better?" he asked.

She nodded and pointed to a remote on the coffee table.

"That turns on the fireplace."

He picked it up and hit the start button, grunting in appreciation as flames flickered to life in the glass fronted firebox.

"Yeah that's a little easier than starting a fire in the forest with wet twigs and branches," he mused.

"No kidding. I dreamed of this very moment," she said, smiling up at him, her accidental breast flash seemingly forgotten.

"I did too," he replied, "though I had to imagine the interior of your living room."

"You mean you didn't peek when you were camping outside earlier this week?" she asked, half teasing, half curious.

"No. I swear. I saw you from a distance. That was it."

She stretched to look outside and was shocked by the severity of the storm.

"I was thinking of calling an ambulance but I don't think they'll make it all the way out here in this weather."

"There is zero visibility right now."

"Would you mind grabbing the cordless phone from the counter and the laminated list of emergency numbers stuck to the fridge please? There's a health line I can call to speak with a nurse."

"No problem," John said, already moving toward the kitchen.

He handed her the phone and numbers. She found the one she needed and dialed. She spent several minutes on the phone, describing her injuries to the person on the line and repeating the first aid instructions she received so that John was aware too. Thanking the person on the line, she said goodbye and disconnected the call.

"The nurse on duty said that the roads are becoming impassable very quickly and the police are already advising people to stay at home. This is about the best we can do right now."

"I feel a little better knowing there's medical advice available if you feel worse."

"I feel better too. Though I'm starving. Are you hungry?" she asked.

"A little," he confessed.

"There's bread in the pantry. And tomato soup. Perhaps you could make grilled cheese sandwiches and heat the soup? I'd do it except I can't move this stupid foot."

"Speaking of that foot, we really should put ice on it. You heard the nurse."

"I know but not yet. I want to warm up a little first. Okay?"

"Okay. But soon Alyson. It will help with swelling and bruising. How's your head feeling?"

"Actually not too bad. I am feeling a bit groggy and tired. I got shampoo in the cut and it hurt like hell. But the dizziness seems to have passed."

"What about your knees?"

"Minor scratches. Is your cheek okay?"

"Yes. Just a little scratch."

"We got off pretty easily all things considered."

"We did," he said, his voice gruff.

"So, how are your culinary skills?"

He laughed, "I'm not much of a cook but I'll do my best."

He walked to the kitchen and stood in front of the island. The kitchen opened up to the living room so Alyson patiently gave him directions on where to find things as he clumsily moved around her space, looking every bit like a fish out of water. Thanks to her verbal coaching, he managed to heat the soup without scorching it and the sandwiches were only slightly burnt on one side. He set their meal out on the huge coffee table. The top of the table looked like it had been carved from a massive piece of driftwood. He liked it. Alyson had good taste.

"You did great," Alyson said around a bite of her sandwich.

"I had a good teacher," he chuckled.

John was certain it was the best meal of his life, though that was probably due to the company he was keeping more so than the food.

"The soup is warming up my insides. I've finally stopped shivering."

"Me too. I'll pay you for the food and shelter," he offered.

"You'll do no such thing," she said, clearly annoyed. "I owe you for saving my life. Big time. The least I can do is offer you a safe place out of the storm and feed you for a few days."

"I'd still prefer to stay in the garage. I don't want to intrude on your space. You've already been incredibly generous."

"John I can't let you stay out there. Please. I have two perfectly good guest rooms in the house. You can chose whichever you'd like. I insist."

He nodded, his cheeks flaming red above the growth of his thick beard. "Thank you, Alyson."

Feeling flustered he stood and started clearing away their dishes, putting everything, even the pans, in the dishwasher as Alyson instructed.

"Would you mind grabbing my oversized comb from my bathroom? It should be in the top drawer of the vanity."

"Of course," he replied, heading for the stairs. He marveled that she was so trusting of him, to let him stay in her home and wander into her private space unchecked. Her wariness and terror from earlier in the day seemed to have turned to blind faith after their shared ordeal. He hoped to God he didn't let her down.

CHAPTER 9

Alyson pulled the towel from her hair, rubbing her long wet tresses between the folds of fabric to absorb as much water as possible. Returning with the comb, John handed it to her and settled on the opposite couch. Alyson noticed him stealing glances at her as she started working through the tangles. The front and sides posed no issue but she winced when the comb grazed the cut at the back of her head. She tried a second time and yelped in pain.

"Damn it. I'll just leave it," she said, tossing the comb onto the coffee table.

John stared at her for a long, silent minute. Standing, he slowly moved to the coffee table and picked up the discarded comb. "I could try," he said, his voice little more than a whisper.

She looked at him wide-eyed, surprised by his offer. She hesitated for several moments and then nodded.

"Okay," she whispered back.

John slowly crossed the few feet between them and stood behind her. He carefully separated the long, wet strands until he located the gash.

"It's bleeding a little again," he said as he gently lifted a hank of her hair. He kept his hand close to her scalp to minimize any tugging while he delicately worked through the knots.

Alyson was afraid to breathe. Joe used to brush her hair sometimes. She always loved it. This reminded her of those times. It seemed such an intimate thing to let a stranger do. Perhaps she was subconsciously starved for human contact, more specifically male contact, because she hadn't even considered saying no. She wondered what John looked like without the dense beard covering his face and the long hair that skimmed his shoulders. It looked thick and was midnight black. His hand moved to the other side of the cut and he repeated the gentle combing until she was completely tangle free.

"Thank you," she said, her voice shaking.

"You're welcome," he gruffly mumbled.

He returned to the couch opposite hers. A long, and not completely comfortable, silence stretched between them. His face was bright red and he looked out of place in the robe and in her home.

"Do you want to use the laundry room?" she offered.

"I would, yes, thank you. I have no idea how to operate the machines though."

She covered the basic directions and he left the room to gather his clothing. Feeling completely drained, Alyson snuggled down into the comfort of her couch and closed her eyes. Just for a moment.

She had no idea how much time had passed but John was shaking her awake. Again.

"Alyson! Wake up. You can't sleep yet. Alyson! Wake up!"

Alyson opened her eyes and smiled in apology. "It's so difficult to stay awake."

"Does your head hurt? Are you dizzy? Nauseated?"

"No. The cut itself feels sore but otherwise I'm okay. The dizziness has passed. I'm just tired now. But you know that could simply be from the excitement of the day. You have to admit, it wasn't an ordinary day."

"That's true. But I can't let you sleep. Not until we know that your symptoms aren't worsening. Let's give it a few hours."

"Okay. I'm happy you're here to keep me in line."

He flashed her one of his full-on smiles and her heart fluttered. She had a feeling he didn't smile very often.

"It's almost dark now," she noted. "I haven't seen the winds this strong in the eight months I've lived here."

"You're not from here?" he asked.

"No. I relocated from Vancouver in March."

"You're not married?"

Alyson paused. Swallowing back tears, she closed her eyes for several long minutes.

"Please do not sleep again."

"I'm not sleeping," she reassured him. Turning to look into the fire she softly uttered the words that always cut her to the core, "I was married. He died."

"I'm sorry."

"It was two years ago," her voice sounded small even to her own ears.

"You don't have to talk about it."

"It's still very difficult. Perhaps you could tell me about you. You mentioned it was a long story. We're not going anywhere."

"I'd rather not if you don't mind."

"Actually I do mind. You saved my life and you're staying in my home. Give me something. Please."

John took a deep breath and looked at her, finally holding her gaze for longer than a moment. "Okay. That's fair. I don't like being around people and I move around a lot."

"Why?"

"I just feel uncomfortable around people."

"You don't seem uncomfortable now."

"You're different. I don't know why but you are."

Alyson quietly watched him as he fidgeted on the couch. His words were creating more questions and not answering the ones she already had.

"Where did you live before you came here?"

"Maine. I spent a couple of years there in a small town on the coast."

"Did you have a house there?"

"I'm homeless, Alyson. I don't have a house. I meant what I said in the forest about everything I own in this world is in my backpack."

"Why Newfoundland?"

"I met a guy who was delivering a boat here. He hired me for the trip."

"So you've always worked on boats?"

"Just while I was in Maine."

"Do you have a wife? Kids?"

"What do you think?"

"Seems like you don't but well, you never know."

"I don't." Despite his words, he seemed uncertain.

"How did you end up homeless?"

"It's complicated. Can we please leave it for now? Please."

"Okay," she agreed. "I think the washer just shut off. You can transfer your clothes to the dryer now." Again she gave him directions on how to use the machine and he set off to the laundry room

Alyson was reeling from the weight of the unanswered questions. She needed a diversion. Perhaps she would change into something a little more comfortable, and less revealing. The only problem was all of her stuff was in her bedroom. She hated asking him to carry her up over the stairs but the thought of him going through her underwear drawer was even less appealing. When he came back into the room she pushed aside her discomfort and asked if he would help her. He didn't hesitate and she couldn't help but smile when he lifted her blanket and all. He didn't seem to want a repeat of the flashed boob incident any more than she did.

He carried her effortlessly to the second floor and she was once again staggered by the intimacy of being in his arms. He was holding her like a lover, not a stranger. He strolled into her bedroom like he had done so a thousand times before, instead of the one time to get her comb. She was relieved when he reached her closet door and stepped inside. Her closet was a massive walk-in with a leather-covered storage bench in the middle.

"There on the bench is fine," she pointed. "I can use the shelves and dressers to lean on to find what I need."

"You're sure. Just tell me what you want and I can bring it to you."

"No! That's fine," Alyson said, a bit abruptly.

John's face flushed bright red as he realized how inappropriate and awkward it would be to select her underwear.

"Right. I'll wait in the hallway. Call out to me when you're ready."

She nodded and watched him walk from the room. She hastily picked out underwear, opting for white cotton with no embellishments. She could feel her own cheeks warming as she rummaged through the vibrant shades of satin and lace. She pulled her warmest flannel pajamas out of a drawer and slipped them on, just as she had imagined doing while stranded in the woods earlier. She tugged on a pair of fleece-lined socks and grimaced as the fabric moved over her injured foot. John would probably insist on icing her ankle soon and he was right, she had to get the swelling down. The bruises that were forming looked nasty and the swollen flesh felt hot under her fingertips. She pushed her arms into a fleece robe and reveled in the feeling of being wrapped in layers of warmth. Her hair had nearly dried as well so that was adding to her comfort. She called out that she was ready and he came inside immediately.

"You look cozy," he grinned, and damn it, his eyes actually sparkled.

There was that flutter again in response to his smile. It was an intensely physical reaction and she wasn't sure how she felt about it.

"I am," she smiled in return.

He crouched to lift her against him and she wrapped her arm around his neck. He paused for a moment and their eyes met. Dammit. This was too intimate. Her fingers accidentally brushed the ends of his shoulder length dark hair. Despite the thickness, it was soft. He smelled really good now and it was disconcerting.

John cleared his throat. "Do you want to go back to the living room?" he asked, his voice even deeper than normal.

She nodded, a little transfixed by his startling eyes. He looked away, breaking the spell, ending the unexpected connection between them, and quickly returned her to the living room. She wondered if she was developing some form of hero worship crush. Bad idea since she knew virtually nothing about him. This was not how she thought her weekend was going to turn out.

"I have an idea," she said as he gently placed her back on the sofa. "Would you mind bringing down my office chair? It has wheels and I could use it as a makeshift wheelchair."

"That's smart thinking. I'll be right back," he said, heading to the second floor. Alyson's eyes were drawn to his well-defined calves showing beneath the robe as he walked across the floor. His bare feet seemed especially erotic. *Stop it*, she mentally chastised, shifting her focus to the fireplace instead of the stairs as he moved out of sight.

A couple of minutes later she heard him coming down the stairs. The chair wasn't small but John handled it like it weighed nothing, much like how he handled her. His strength seemed to come from the effort of survival, not from some fancy gym membership. She felt a quiet respect for that.

"Let's try this out," he suggested as he positioned the chair close enough to the couch that she could transfer herself into it without too much difficulty. It moved a little sluggishly on the rug spanning the room between the sofas, but once she hit the hardwood it was easy to propel herself forward with her good foot. She rolled into the kitchen.

"Would you like tea or coffee?" she asked.

"I'd love coffee," he said, walking into the kitchen behind her.

She flipped the power button on a fancy looking coffee maker and rolled into the oversized pantry. She grabbed two coffee pods and the bottle of Irish cream whiskey from the bottom shelf.

"The mugs are in that cupboard there," she pointed. "Do you want a shot of this in your coffee?" she asked holding up the bottle.

"I don't drink."

"No worries." She splashed a generous serving of the liqueur in one of the mugs he had placed on the counter.

"That smells good," he leaned in closer to inhale the sweetness.

"Sure you don't want a shot?"

"Maybe a small one," he grinned.

She poured about an ounce into the second mug and popped a coffee pod in the machine.

"How convenient," he murmured as the rich brown liquid gurgled into the mug.

She handed him the mug. He took a long sip and groaned with pleasure. She grinned as she prepared her own mug.

"Damn. That is good," he smiled, obviously enjoying the brew.

"You've never tried that before?"

John looked at her, shyly smiling. "No. Not many luxuries when you live like I do."

"Sorry. I didn't mean to be insensitive."

"You weren't. Not at all. Here let me grab your mug for you."

He carried their hot beverages back to the living room, setting them down on coasters. Alyson rolled in behind him on the office chair, enjoying the modicum of independence. The wind was howling outside, shaking the house with its intensity at times. She was so grateful to be safe at home. They settled onto sofas and she smiled as she watched him lift the mug to his face and deeply inhale the aroma of the strong brew.

"My God that smells so good," he sighed.

"You really appreciate the little things, huh?" she asked.

"This isn't a little thing. This is manna from the gods," he grinned.

She lifted her own mug to her lips, watching him in fascination as he continued to savour his coffee. It made her realize that she rarely tasted anything any more. She ate not for pleasure but to fuel her body. It was just one of many casualties she had suffered living life on autopilot since Joe's death. She took a long sip from her own mug and let the rich flavours roll over her tongue. Damn! It was better than she remembered.

CHAPTER 10

John pulled his clean clothes from the dryer and hastily shrugged into a pair of worn jeans and a long sleeved tee with frayed cuffs. The house was warm so he skipped socks, relishing the indulgence of going barefoot. He had consulted with Alyson about whether it was okay to wash and dry his sleeping bag, too. She said the appliances were heavy duty and could handle the bulk, as long as the bag could be laundered. He found the tag with instructions but the print was too fine. His vision blurred and he couldn't focus to read it. He pushed the sleeping bag into a laundry basket so it wouldn't drip all over the floor. If it couldn't be laundered, chances are it was too wet to be saved at this point. He toted the basket into the living room to ask for her help reading the label.

She hesitated for a moment and then softly asked, "Is it really the print, or can you read?"

He answered her with equal kindness, "I may be homeless but I'm not illiterate."

"Sorry," she said, genuine regret in her eyes.

"No. It's okay. I can see why you might think that."

"You should see an optometrist. Get your eyes checked. You probably need reading glasses."

"It's on my to-do list," he quipped, his fingers making air quotes, hoping to make her smile. The truth was optometrists cost money and he did not have insurance. Hell he didn't have a driver's license or a social security number either. He didn't even have an identity, only the one he had created for himself. He wondered what she would think of that.

"Yup. This is machine washable. You're good to go."

"Thank you. I really appreciate this."

"It's nothing," she smiled.

He returned to the laundry room, popped his sleeping bag into the washing machine and finished folding his meager items of clothing. He inhaled their fresh from the dryer scent. Since his pack was still wet, he stacked them in a neat pile on the laundry room counter.

"Can I get you anything?" he asked as he walked back into the living room.

"Maybe a cup of tea. And please help yourself to whatever you'd like."

"Thanks, I'd love another coffee."

"The coffee pods and tea are in the pantry, third shelf."

He was starting to navigate her kitchen with a familiarity that both pleased and bothered him. It was nice having such a beautiful place to stay, if only for a couple of days. He appreciated Alyson's hospitality and her company. On the other hand, it would be difficult to walk away. He felt strangely at home here and completely at ease with her. That was new territory for him.

He handed her the mug of tea and sipped from his own as he walked toward the window. The room felt warm and cozy and he sent a silent prayer of gratitude to the universe for the twist of fate that led him here.

"It isn't letting up at all," he observed, looking out into a blizzard that obliterated the outside world. He could see her reflection in the glass and he stayed there for long minutes, pretending to watch the storm. He liked watching her forehead furrow as she blew across the surface of her hot tea and the half smile that played across her mouth after each sip, as though the act of drinking brought her joy. She was incredible.

"Do you work?" he asked, returning to the couch and sitting across from her.

"Not any more. I was an editor. I think I may be ready to take on a couple of assignments though."

"Do you have any family or friends here?"

"No. They're all in Vancouver. My mom and dad and my younger sister, Sydney. My best friend, Lois lives there as well. What about your parents? Siblings?"

"I don't have any."

"Really? There's no one?"

"There's no one."

"I'm sorry, John. That must be tough."

"It is what it is. I don't think about it too much."

The power dipped and the lights dimmed as an especially violent gust of wind shook the house.

"Looks like it's actually getting worse out there," Alyson sighed, lifting her mug to her lips.

"Should I round up extra blankets and candles or something, in case the power goes out?"

"No that's okay. The house has a built in generator. Apparently it powers the blower on the gas fireplace, the refrigerator, freezer, several outlets and some of the lights. The stove is gas anyway so we should be quite comfortable. I've never actually tested the generator but I'm assuming it will work. It's supposed to start automatically in a power failure."

"Is there extra fuel?"

"It's tied to the propane tanks out back."

"That's impressive."

"Yeah. I didn't really give it much thought when I bought the house but I have a feeling we'll appreciate that feature before this storm has finished with us."

"So you bought this great big house just for you?"

"Yeah. Seems extravagant, doesn't it?" she shrugged and flashed him a self-deprecating smile. "This might sound crazy but I was indifferent to the house. I was attracted to the remoteness. And I loved the view."

"I can't imagine having all of this space. I'm used to living in an eighty square foot room at the best of times or my tent, smaller again."

"You must have had a home at some point?" she gently prodded.

"I suppose."

"Well that's vague. You must know if you had a home over the span of your lifetime."

He paused for a long time before softly saying, "I can't remember."

"You can't remember? How could you forget something like that?"

"I'm not sure."

"Are there other things you can't remember?"

"Trust me Alyson, you do not want to know the answer to that question."

"What if I do?"

John groaned and walked back to the window.

"I'll be gone in a day or two. It won't matter. Speaking of which, is there anyone who can stay with you until your foot heals?"

Alyson shook her head, looking small and alone huddled under the blanket, "There's no one. But I'll manage."

"How on earth will you manage? You can't even get up and down the stairs."

"I may have you help me move some of my things down to the guest room on this floor tomorrow. It will make it easier to shower and change."

"I can certainly do that. But I don't think you should be alone until you can get that foot checked out."

"Please don't worry. The storm will probably last for a couple of days anyway. You're stuck with me until then."

John looked at her and cleared his throat, "May I ask you a question?"

"Yes. Of course."

"Did I really scare you this morning? On the trail? You looked terrified when you saw me."

Alyson smiled, "Yes. You did. You were unexpected. I hike that trail almost every day and I've never met anyone out there before. You seemed big and well, just unexpected."

"Big, smelly, scary," John grinned.

"You do smell much better now."

"I'm grateful. Believe me."

"I know you are."

They smiled at each other. The silence and the moment stretched out between them. John took a deep breath, suddenly feeling hyper aware of the vulnerable woman sitting less than ten feet away.

"We really need to get some ice on that ankle," his voice was even gruffer than normal. "Do you have an ice pack?"

"No, but there are a couple of packages of frozen peas in the freezer. They'll do."

"I'll grab one," he went to the kitchen and rummaged in her freezer.

He elevated her foot on a pillow and draped it with a folded dishtowel before placing the peas on top.

"Twenty minutes on and twenty off," she said, wiggling back against the arm of the couch and noting the time on the large clock that hung on the opposite wall of the living room.

"How's your head doing?"

"I have a slight headache but no dizziness or nausea."

"That's good. We might actually be able to sleep later."

"I would love to take a nap."

"I'll want to wake you every hour or so."

"We'll set an alarm then."

"Do you need Tylenol or something?"

"Actually, yes, please. It might help with the throbbing in my foot. It's in the main bathroom closet, second shelf I think."

"Need anything else from upstairs?"

"My e-reader, please. It's on the nightstand next to my bed. There are hundreds of books in the study if you want to grab one."

"Thanks. I will."

He took the stairs, two at a time and grabbed the meds and her fancy book reader. He avoided looking at her bed. Best to leave those thoughts buried in the back of his mind. Her study had floor to ceiling built-in bookcases and there were literally hundreds of books. He didn't want to take too long so he pulled a random title from the nearest shelf. It looked like a murder mystery. He shook his head in an amazement. This day felt like a dream. Granted part of it had been nightmarish but this part was the stuff of his fantasies.

They settled in a companionable silence, reading and sipping their hot beverages. He felt like he had landed in the middle of someone else's life. If someone had told him a couple of nights ago when he had camped in the woods behind her house that he would be temporarily staying here, he would have laughed at them. Being on this side of her window felt surreal. He glanced over at her now and then. She seemed quite absorbed in her book, although once he caught her staring at him. Poor thing was probably trying to figure out what to make of him. He smiled at her and she smiled in return. He was starting to wish for all sorts of impossible things. He wanted to be worthy of someone like her. No. That wasn't it exactly. He wanted to be worthy of *her*. He wanted to be able to offer her something, everything. These were unchartered waters for him and he had no idea how to navigate the course ahead.

He should tell her the truth. She was being so kind to him and she deserved to know who he was, who she was offering shelter to in the storm. She glanced up at him as though sensing that he was watching her.

"I don't know who I am," he blurted.

"Sorry?" she asked, her eyes widening at the unexpected confession.

"You asked what else I might not remember. The truth is, I don't have any memory of who I am. For as long as I can remember I've been homeless and alone with a strong compulsion to keep moving."

Alyson stared at him, clearly astonished by what he had just revealed. She looked as though she was pondering her words carefully before she finally spoke.

"Do you know how long you've been homeless?"

"Not really. Sometimes my memory is still fuzzy. It's hard to explain. It's like I know I've been somewhere or done something but the details won't come into focus."

"That sounds horrifying. Have you seen a doctor?"

"No."

"Why on earth not?"

"I don't have insurance or money for doctors and testing. I don't have identification. I don't even know my name. I refer to myself as John Smith because it is a little less cheesy than John Doe. Everyone expects a name."

"So your name might not even be John?"

"No," he held her gaze. It was difficult because he saw all of the questions and doubts that were flooding her mind.

"What's your earliest memory?"

"I can remember the St. Louis Cardinals winning the World Series in 2006. I was at a diner in St. Louis and everyone was watching the game on a small TV mounted above the coffee bar. The place went mad when they won. Well, everyone except me. I was eating a ham sandwich and drinking a cup of coffee and I can remember spending my last five bucks on that meal."

"That's ten years ago. You can't remember anything from before then?"

"Nothing clearly, no. There are bits and pieces but nothing that I can link to a date."

"And you just keep moving? How do you find work without identification?"

"I find jobs that pay cash. Usually the crappy jobs no one else wants. But they keep me alive."

"Why not settle down somewhere?"

"People make me uncomfortable." He paused, knowing this was the scariest missing piece of his puzzle. "I have this strong sense that I'm running from something or someone but I don't know what. Or who."

"Seriously? That's rather unsettling. Do you think someone is trying to hurt you in some way?" Her face paled. "Do you think you've done something wrong?"

"I don't know, Alyson. God I hope not but I really don't know."

She looked ashen and he'd bet his pack and all its contents that she was shaking like a leaf.

"I don't feel like I could possibly hurt someone. I hope that makes you feel better."

"I'm not sure how I should feel. I'm sorry. It's just a bit of a shock hearing all of this. My God. What if you've committed some horrible crime and you're running from the police? Is that possible?"

He swallowed down the fear and dread because he had wondered the same thing. Countless times. "Anything is possible."

CHAPTER 11

Alyson felt blindsided. He didn't know his actual identity? He had memory issues? Was he being honest or was he playing her? He said he had camped in her back yard a couple of nights ago and made it seem coincidental. Was it really? What if he had been stalking her? Maybe he found out about the generous settlement she received from Joe's estate. She was independently wealthy and maybe he was ambushing her and this was some elaborate hostage scenario. It made sense in a bizarre, off-the wall, only-happens-in-the-movies way. She would be worth much more to him alive, than dead. That might explain why he worked so hard to save her life. Or maybe his plan was even more elaborate and devious than that. Maybe his intention was to sweep her off her feet, marry her and then he'd be entitled to half her net worth. Unless there was a pre-nup. Or shit, unless he killed her, then he'd get it all.

Her imagination had kicked into overdrive and she could feel a panic attack building. The sound of his voice, soft as a whisper in the vast expanse of the room, startled her back to the present.

"I can't even imagine what thoughts are racing through that beautiful head of yours right now but I swear, I would never do anything to harm you."

She met his gaze and was crushed by the look of sincerity and vulnerability in his eyes. She thought of how he had wrapped the tree limb in his shirt before splinting her leg. She thought of the dozens of little things he had done for her in the few short hours since she had met him. She wanted to believe him. She really did.

"I want to accept that's true. It's just quite a bit to absorb."

"I know. I'm sorry for blurting it out like that. I just suddenly couldn't stand that you didn't know. I needed you to know. I've never told anyone before."

"John, you need to get medical help. Soon. You need to tell the police about your situation. They might be able to help."

"I will. I promise."

"Why haven't you gone to the police before?"

"I was afraid of what I'd find out."

"You're not afraid now?"

"Even more so. But for the first time I want to know what I'm facing."

She couldn't help wonder if that had something to do with her. Maybe their harrowing hike today had shifted paradigms inside both of them. She pulled herself up into the office chair and clumsily wheeled herself to the washroom off the mudroom, declining his offer of help. She needed a few moments alone. She caught a glimpse of her reflection in the mirror hanging on the back of the washroom door and was surprised to see how pale she looked. But then, it had been a hellish day.

Once again, she second guessed her decision to live in such an isolated area. She knew the police wouldn't be able to make it here in the storm but should she call and at least alert them to the situation? He really hadn't given her any reason to think she was in danger but should she trust that? The blizzard looked worse than anything she could even imagine, certainly worse than any other storm she had ever experienced. With winds that high there were bound to be snowdrifts too deep to drive through. The nurse had even said people were being advised to stay home. The snow clearing equipment had probably even been removed from the streets by now. She'd turn on the TV when she returned to the living room to see what was happening outside the walls of her house. With any luck, the storm would peter out soon and life could return to normal. She took a deep breath and maneuvered the chair through the hallway, slowly making her way back to the living room.

"Are you okay?" he asked, his face etched with concern.

"I'm fine," she replied, a little more tersely than she had intended.

"Alyson do you want me to leave? I'll completely understand if you do."

"I can't turn you out in this storm. It's brutal outside. It's even worse than it was half an hour ago."

"I could stay in the garage. You could lock the door from your end."

"If you really wanted access to the house you could easily smash a window. What would that prove?"

"I don't want you scared and uncomfortable in your own home."

"Too late for that. But please, be honest with me about one thing, okay?"

"Of course. I'm being honest with you about everything. So please, ask me anything," she detected a flash of hurt in his eyes.

"Why were you camping behind my house? Were you spying on me? Stalking me?"

"No! Of course not! That was pure coincidence. I swear. I was hoping to find an abandoned shed or house in the area that I could use for a while. I wasn't spying. It's just when I saw you I couldn't quite make myself look away. I'm sorry."

"I want to believe you."

"It's difficult. I know."

"Yeah. It is."

They both paused, neither sure what to say next.

"I'll get the other peas. Your twenty minutes are up."

Alyson watched him walk out of the room and couldn't control the tremors that were shaking her entire body. She wanted to believe him, and for the most part she did, but there was this little voice of caution that sounded suspiciously like her mother's voice, buzzing in her head telling her to be careful.

"Thank you," she said as he gently removed her sock to look at her ankle and then pulled it back in place before positioning the makeshift ice pack.

"It's really bruising but the swelling doesn't seem quite as bad. That's good at least."

"Yeah," she said, reaching for the TV remote and switching to the local news, ending the necessity for idle chatter.

The storm was even worse that she had feared. Police were advising that roads were impassable and it was too dangerous to operate snow clearing equipment. The storm was much bigger than had been forecasted, being fed from three different systems that had converged. They were calling it the perfect storm. She had a different phrase for it in mind. She left the television on, the voices of the newscasters morphing into the drone of some mindless sit-com interspersed with canned audience laughter. None of it registered. Her head was pounding from the effort of trying to make sense of everything John had told her. It was quite a bit to process after the ordeal of being injured and coming closer than she'd care to admit to dying in that storm today. She hadn't died because of John. He was the sole reason that she was still here. She gave a sigh of reluctant acceptance. No matter what he had just confided, he had shown her nothing but kindness. She couldn't kick him out and so she had to trust that his word was good. They may as well make the most of it.

"Do you know how to play Scrabble?" she asked, hoping he would recognize and accept the olive branch she offered.

"If I say I can't remember, I hope it will make you smile," he said, tilting his head and smiling his gratitude.

Great. He had a charming side too. "I'll refresh your memory then. The Scrabble board is in the closet just off the dining room if you wouldn't mind getting it."

"Not at all."

She set up the board on the couch and he settled on the end opposite her. She was sitting with her feet propped on a pillow on the coffee table sans frozen peas for the next twenty minutes. She explained the basic rules of the game and within half a dozen moves he had established a substantial lead.

"I think I've been had," she groaned, feigning despair.

"Nope. First time playing. I swear. At least that I can remember."

"Well between the luck of your tiles and your impressive vocabulary, you're whipping my butt."

"I'm not sure where those words are coming from," he admitted.

"Well I don't think there is any way you could be cheating so enjoy the victory."

Their lighthearted banter was exactly what they needed to diffuse the heaviness that hung over them since his confession. He won by an impressive fifty points. It was getting late so she challenged him to a rematch after dinner. They paused to heat a couple of the gourmet frozen dinners from the deli for their evening meal. Despite the rumbling in her stomach, Alyson couldn't force herself to eat much. John cleared his plate though and she wondered when he had last eaten a decent meal before today.

"What the heck do you eat when you're in the middle of nowhere like this?"

"It's been a while since I've camped out as long as I have here but I pack dehydrated foods, beef jerky, dried fruits. Stuff that doesn't take up too much room in my pack. Though with the temperatures so low, I've been wearing most of my clothes so that freed up some space. I hunt if necessary. I was actually heading back to St. John's today when our paths crossed. I'd pretty much exhausted my provisions and it was getting too cold to camp."

"Please help yourself to anything in the pantry or fridge. You're welcome to whatever you want." She didn't ask him what he hunted. She didn't want to know the gory details.

"My stomach isn't used to heavy food so I have to be careful about what I reintroduce into my diet. The coffee is such a treat though. I only had room for a small bottle of instant and despite using it sparingly, I ran out a few days ago."

"I mean it. Feel free to help yourself."

"Thank you, Alyson."

"Are you planning to rent a place St. John's?" she asked.

"Yes. For the next few months at least, assuming I can find work."

"I can help you get to the city after the storm."

"Thanks but I don't mind walking. It helps me stay in shape."

She decided to let it go for now. They started another game of Scrabble and this time she won but by a very narrow margin. He was a challenging opponent and she enjoyed that. Even though he had no memory of his early adult life, he was clearly well educated and well read. It just made him more of a mystery. The power dipped a couple of more times and finally went out. They held their breath as the generator kicked in, exactly as the realtor had promised. Only a couple of the lights stayed on, but they were enough to break the darkness. The fireplace blower provided some warmth but with the high ceilings and open concept design of the first floor, it couldn't keep ahead of the cold and the room got chilly surprisingly fast. John rounded up extra blankets and they each snuggled under a pile of blankets on their respective couches. They set an alarm for thirty minutes to see how easily Alyson woke from sleep and when she stirred at the sound of the alarm itself, they decided to sleep for a longer stretch. Alyson snuggled down under the covers, so happy to finally give in to the exhaustion that had seeped into every pore. Her last thought as she drifted off was that she half jokingly, half seriously hoped he didn't murder her in her sleep.

CHAPTER 12

John couldn't sleep. He was weary but wired, too. He felt good about coming clean with Alyson, even though he knew the truth had scared the crap out of her. He couldn't fault her for that. It was a hell of a load to dump on someone. He admired her bravado and graciousness more than he could measure. He didn't like people as a rule but even if he had let people in, he had a feeling that people like Alyson Fisher were few and far between. She was accepting and kind and willing to give him the benefit of the doubt in this unusual situation. He owed her an incredible debt of gratitude. He would figure out some way to repay her for her kindness and acceptance after this storm blew over.

He turned to watch her sleep. He was moved by the depth of her beauty. Even with dark shadows beneath her closed eyes and her skin pale from the trauma of the day, she was the loveliest woman he had ever seen. Her lashes were long and thick, fanning across her upper cheeks. Her full lips parted in her sleep and she sighed deeply. The covers were pulled up tightly and tucked under her chin, hiding the gentle curves of her body. That was probably a blessing in disguise. He had been fighting an erection for the better part of the day. She hadn't seemed to notice, thank God. No need to freak her out completely. The last thing he needed her thinking was that he was some sex-starved deviant.

He wondered what it would be like to be partnered with someone like Alyson. To live in a house like this with her. To wake every morning to her beautiful smile. To have the right to kiss her and hold her and love her. To have children with her. To grow old with her. She would never want to be with someone like him. He knew that. He had nothing to offer. He probably had ghosts in his past waiting to haunt him once he started digging. There might even be monsters in there waiting to eviscerate him. She deserved better than that. She deserved better than him. Still, for the first time in memory, he wanted to dream. He wanted to imagine. He wanted to soak enough of her in over the next few days to fuel his dreams and fantasies for a long time to come. He was certain he would remember her long after she had forgotten him.

He closed his eyes and willed himself to remember. Something. Anything from his past. Had there been a wife? Kids? Surely not. How on earth could he have forgotten a family? But then, he had forgotten his own identity. He tried to focus on remembering beyond the haze of that World Series game in 2006. The only image that came to his mind was a busy city street. Tall buildings. Crowds of people moving hurriedly. Absolutely no help. That could be virtually any city anywhere in the world.

Alyson had asked him if he was American because he had said mile instead of kilometer. He did think in miles. Inches. Pounds. So perhaps he was American. He had no reason to think otherwise at this point. He didn't seem to have a discernable accent; no southern drawl or distinctive northeastern dialect. He worked through a list of possible occupations in his head to see if he would identify with one, if something would spark in his memory. Nothing. He did the same thing with names, hoping that some name, perhaps his own, would flash through his mind and help him remember. It was an exercise he did often but always with the same result.

No jolt of recognition. No lifting of the fog that blanketed his brain.

Maybe he was better off not remembering. Maybe whatever had happened in his past was so horrible that he should leave well enough alone. Maybe there was a physical problem. He wondered how much a doctor's visit and testing might cost. He had saved up almost ten thousand dollars from his two years working in Maine. If he had an established identity he would have made four times that amount. As it was, hiding that much money in his socks at the bottom of his pack was taking up quite a bit of room.

He watched the alarm count down the two hours and as it beeped, Alyson stirred, though it took her a little longer to wake than before. She had probably just been in a deeper sleep.

"Hi," she said stretching. "Did you sleep?"

"A little," he said rather than admitting he hadn't slept at all.

"Feel free to take one of the guest rooms if you want. The couch is probably too short for you."

"I'm okay here, thanks. Do you want to go to your bedroom? I can help you."

"No it's fine. Plus it's warmer down here."

"Good. It will make it easier to check that you're waking when the alarm sounds if you're close by."

"Okay. You should really sleep too, though. I'm counting on you to dig us out once this blizzard stops."

"No worries. I will happily dig us out."

"Good night, John."

"Good night, Alyson. Sweet dreams."

CHAPTER 13

Alyson screamed as the wild dog sank its teeth into her ankle. She tried to push it off her but it wouldn't let go. She kept screaming for help and tried to run away but she was frozen in place.

"Alyson. Wake up. You're dreaming. It's okay. It's okay."

John's voice finally penetrated her terror and roused her from the nightmare. She was crying and shaking.

"It's okay. You're safe. You were having a bad dream."

"There was a wild dog or coyote or something and it was biting me."

"It was just a dream."

"Sorry. I feel so stupid."

"Don't. You've had an incredibly stressful day. No wonder you had a bad dream. Do you want something to drink?"

"Just water please."

"Coming right up."

Alyson tried to compose herself. She couldn't stop shaking. She felt chilled and wondered if it was just the shock of the nightmare or if it was that cold in the house with the power out.

"Hey are you cold? I can't stop shaking," she said as she accepted the glass of water from him and took a sip.

"It is chilly here but not freezing. Do you want me to get more blankets?"

"No but maybe we should move the couch closer to the fireplace."

"You stay there and I'll move the other one over."

He repositioned the couch he had been using and folded back the blankets that had been covering him. She pulled the office chair next to her.

"I could carry you," he offered.

She felt completely drained and quickly accepted his offer, "Thank you."

He felt warm and strong and she selfishly wanted to hoard his body heat. Plus it wasn't entirely unpleasant being in his arms. He settled her on the couch and pulled the covers over her.

"Is that better?" he asked.

"I think so, yes. Thank you."

"No problem." He moved to the couch she had just vacated.

Alyson hesitated for a moment and then said, "Come share this couch. You'll be warmer. And I'll be warmer, too."

"Are you sure?"

"Yes, I am."

He sat on the opposite end of the couch, carefully pulling her feet onto his lap.

"Is this okay?" he asked, seeming to belatedly realize how presumptuous it was to touch her with such unguarded familiarity.

"Yes. This is much warmer. Are you comfortable?"

"Yes. This is perfect," he smiled.

"I can't believe that a storm this bad is happening so early in the season. I hope it isn't indicative of a nasty winter ahead."

"It's unlike anything I have experienced or could have imagined."

"Me too."

He paused for a long moment. "May I ask you something? Personal?"

"Sure. I might choose not to answer though."

"That's fair." Again he paused. "You said that your husband passed away two years ago. You haven't met anyone else?"

"No. I haven't been looking."

"That's a long time to be alone."

"You sound like my family and Lois."

"Sorry. I'm being inappropriate. It's none of my business."

Alyson glanced at him and then looked into the fire. "The truth is, I wanted to die myself after losing Joe. He was the love of my life and his death devastated me. Nearly destroyed me. Moving here was my escape from my loved ones' well-meaning attempts to set me up and help me find love again. Except they were doomed to fail. I don't think it exists for me anymore."

"That's a sad thought, Alyson."

"I know. I've accepted it. I did have a bit of an epiphany in the forest today though. Before you found me I realized how I've been wasting my time. Wasting my life since Joe died. Just because I don't want a man in my life doesn't mean I should live a shallow life. I promised myself I'd try harder."

"Good for you. That's really great."

"Are you going to try harder too? Figure out who you are? What you're running from?" she asked.

He held her gaze for a dozen heart beats and nodded. "Yes. I will try harder too."

"Good," she smiled, settling back against the couch.

They stared at the fire for a while, the silence from within the room wrapping around them. Outside the winds raged and howled and sometimes gusts shook the house. The windows were completely covered with snow so it was impossible to tell how much had fallen. With winds like this, some areas would have bare ground and others would have drifts several feet high. It would make snow clearing especially challenging. Alyson had a standing contract with a local man who had a plough on his truck. He also cleared the walks and mowed her rather expansive lawn in the summer.

She wondered how many days would pass before they could drive to St. John's. She really wanted to get her foot and head checked. If she couldn't bear weight on her foot by then she wouldn't be able to drive. She wondered if John knew how to drive a car. She didn't bother to ask. She was enjoying the silence too much. She was enjoying the feeling of having her feet on a man's lap again. It had been such a long time. The last man to hold her feet on his lap had been Joe. The last man to kiss her romantically had been Joe. The last man to make love to her had been Joe.

She closed her eyes but was afraid to sleep. She didn't want to have any more bad dreams. John stretched his blanket covered feet closer to the fire and when she glanced at him, he was resting his head against the back of the couch but his face was turned away from her. She assumed he was probably trying to sleep.

She stared at the fire until her eyes grew heavy and drifted shut. Her sleep was dreamless this time. Deep and peaceful. She wasn't sure how long she had slept or what had stirred her awake. Her leg was cramping a little, maybe that's what had roused her. She shifted slightly and froze when her foot brushed against something. Hard. *Oh sweet Jesus.* He had an erection. Was he asleep? Was he dreaming? Worse, was he awake? She slowly moved her foot in the other direction, hoping she wouldn't wake him. Hoping she would not have to face the embarrassment of another awkward moment with this veritable stranger.

He didn't stir and she released the breath she had been holding as she gently settled her foot on his lower thigh. She wondered how long it had been since he had been with a woman. Did he have a girl in every town he'd visited? Had he left a string of broken hearts clear across the country? The continent? She wondered yet again what he looked like under all that hair. His eyes were incredible. She actually avoided looking directly into his eyes as much as possible because she was afraid if she lingered too long, she would get lost in his gaze. Such a corny thought but the fear was real. She wondered if he had been without female companionship as long as she had been without Joe. He seemed to be a virile man, surely he would have taken lovers over the last ten years.

Holy shit. What if he really did have a wife and kids waiting for him somewhere? He said he didn't but he had forgotten other things. Perhaps he had forgotten them too. It was almost unimaginable. Surely if he had a family they would have reported him missing. And if he had been some sort of fugitive, with the immediacy and reach of social media, he would have been recognized and apprehended by now. She clung to that thought. She couldn't imagine harbouring a criminal. She couldn't imagine that he was capable of any ill-deed. He treated her with respect and kindness, unfailingly. She had to focus on that.

He shifted and came awake with a sudden start. He looked at Alyson and seemed flustered to realize that she was awake. She felt him discretely tug at his jeans under the covers and she couldn't help but grin at his obvious discomfort.

"How long did I sleep?" he asked.

"I'm not sure. I fell asleep too."

He stretched to see the clock on the far wall. "Looks like we passed another couple of hours. You doing okay? Warm enough?"

"Yes. Are you doing okay?" she asked, trying to hide the grin.

"I'm fine," he said. "Never better." His hand absently stroked her uninjured foot as he drifted back to sleep. Alyson wasn't feeling quite as smug about his physical discomfort now; not when his innocent caress was wreaking havoc on her own long dormant libido. She forced herself to think of Joe. She forced herself to let the pain of being without him seep into every ounce of her being. The rush of sadness was almost enough to displace her growing arousal. She could simply move her foot. She should probably move her foot.

Or she could close her eyes and savour the contact.

CHAPTER 14

The storm raged all through the weekend and into Monday night. The power showed no signs of returning so John moved the second sofa closer to the fireplace, positioning it parallel to the other one. They spent most of their time in the living room with their feet close to the fireplace. It was cozy and with extra layers of clothing, they were comfortable. Sunday was a pleasant blur of Scrabble matches, simple meals, lighthearted banter and long dozes. Alyson had resisted asking him any more about his past and he was grateful for that, though she did mention a handful of times that he had to seek help after the storm. John couldn't remember being happier in his life. He knew it wouldn't last. He was living on borrowed time and he would be moving on very soon, but the precious hours carved out with Alyson were a blessing.

Late Sunday evening they were settled on the couch, both focusing on a particularly intense Scrabble match, when the shrill ringing of the phone broke their concentration. Alyson reached for the phone on the end table next to her.

"It's my mother," she sighed before picking up.

"I'll leave," he offered.

"No need," she said as lifted the receiver.

He went into the kitchen to make them a snack. It was impossible not to hear Alyson's side of the conversation. Her mother had obviously heard about the storm and was checking on her. Interestingly though, Alyson didn't tell her about her injury on the trail. Or about him. She kept the call brief with a promise to catch up again in a few days.

"She worries too much," she said as she ended the call.

"She must miss you."

"I know she does. And I feel a little guilty for moving so far away."

"Will you see them for Christmas?"

"They want me to fly out but I really don't feel ready to return to Vancouver quite yet."

"Won't you be lonely here by yourself."

"Lonely is my default, John. I'm used to it. You must feel lonely too."

"It's weird but I don't usually, no. Perhaps it's because I can't remember. You have your memories to comfort and torment you."

"Hmph. Memories to comfort and torment. God you nailed that."

"The night I camped out in your woods and saw you on the upstairs deck?"

"Yeah?"

"I could feel your loneliness that night. And it was the first time I could remember feeling lonely myself. It was an odd feeling."

"You could tell that I was lonely just from observing me on the deck?"

"There was something about the way you were huddled inside of the sweater you were wearing. Something so sad and lonesome about the way you were looking out over the ocean. I'm pretty sure you were crying. At that moment I wished that it had been possible to offer you comfort. A fanciful thought but it stayed with me all night."

"You mean you dreamed about me?"

John could feel his face flaming as he realized what he had just admitted. "Yes, Alyson. You haunted my dreams that night. A dark haired beauty with sad eyes. At least they were sad in my dreams."

She mulled that over for a while, not saying anything but she didn't look completely unhappy about the thought. He was relieved that she didn't ask him about the specifics of the dream. That would have made both of them extremely uncomfortable.

The storm finally started to abate Monday evening. The snow stopped and the winds started to settle. It was too dark outside to assess the damage but without the wind pummeling the house, the living room started to heat up.

When they woke on Tuesday morning the sun seemed extraordinarily bright against the backdrop of white outside the windows. The storm had finally passed and from what they could see, there were drifts of snow nearly as tall as the house. They took a tentative peek out the front door and were astounded to see a wall of snow. It would probably take most of the day to dig out. John wished Alyson's ankle was stronger so they could go outside and play in the winter wonderland. He couldn't remember the last time he had felt the urge to play and be carefree. He smiled as he tucked the impulse away to take out and cherish at a later, lonelier time. After he left her.

At least she was able to bear weight on her foot for short periods now. That was progress, though he was concerned that she would overdo it and exacerbate her injury. At his insistence, she stayed off her feet as much as possible, though clearly she didn't like being tended on or catered to. Well tough. He took great pleasure in caring for her so for the next couple of stolen days he was committed to doing exactly that.

They worked together to cook a hearty breakfast of bacon, eggs and toast. He enjoyed being close to her. It was easy to pretend they were sharing a regular day and they were a regular couple. Dangerous thinking. Alyson claimed he needed lots of protein and energy to face the piles of snow outside so they cooked extra. His favourite part was the freshly squeezed orange juice. He loved oranges. After their meal, she showed him where the snow blower was stored in the garage and how to operate it. He dressed in his newly laundered jacket, dry boots with bright pink laces borrowed from her runners and a pair of insulated gloves that Alyson had bought for her dad for Christmas but insisted he use. He dug his way out of the side door of the garage and started the laborious task of removing the towering banks of snow that had drifted around her house, blocking doorways and burying the walkways. Alyson watched him from inside and he was surprised by how much he enjoyed that she waved to him now and then.

In the past ten years he had avoided contact with people as much as possible. He hadn't formed friendships and his only acquaintances were the crew on the fishing boat and the bookshop owner. He hadn't had any romantic interests and had not encountered anyone who remotely enticed him. He'd even wondered at times if he was asexual. It was almost as though celibacy was his default state. This woman was stirring some primordial urge in him to possess. He was overcome with the desire to make her his in some way. In every way. It was startling in its intensity and disconcertingly foreign to him. He stuffed the impulse in a tightly covered box in the back of his mind and tried to focus on the task at hand. Whenever he looked up to see her smiling face watching him though, he just wanted to march into the house, pull her into his arms and kiss the stuffing out of her. Damn it, he needed relief or a long cold shower. Something. This woman was driving him crazy, in the best possible way.

It did take him the better part of the day to clear the snow from the walkways around the house and the driveway outside of the garage doors. Alyson said the plough-guy would clear the rest of the driveway after he took care of his more critical customers. John didn't care if it took the guy days to get around to her place. Now that they were relatively certain she wasn't seriously injured, he would happily stay stuck here with her indefinitely.

The power had been restored by mid-afternoon and when he returned to the house for a break it was warm and cozy inside. A few hours later they heard the roar of a diesel engine and the scraping of metal on pavement. The plough-guy had arrived. The driveway was cleared. The local news stations were reporting that the main roads were also open. This was it. Tomorrow he would leave. She no longer needed him and he would only be in the way staying here. He felt an overwhelming sadness and wasn't even aware that he had retreated into himself. Alyson had insisted on cooking him lasagna, doing all of the prep work at the counter while sitting on a barstool. It was delicious but it was tinged with melancholy.

"You okay?" she asked, picking up on his silence as they ate dinner.

"Yes. Of course. Just planning what comes next. I'd like to ride to the city with you tomorrow if that's okay. See if I can find a place to stay."

"Sure. If that's what you want."

His eyes flew to hers. "It's my only option."

"No it isn't. I've been thinking. Why don't you stay here for a while longer? Just until you can get medical help and talk to the police. You're more than welcome, if you want."

"That's incredibly generous of you but I don't want to impose."

"You're not. I'm offering. Plus my foot is still tenuous and you make a great gopher."

He looked at her for a long moment, a range of emotions flitting across his face. "Thank you. That means a great deal to me. But just for a few more days, until I figure out a plan forward."

"Sounds good. Up for a Scrabble match or are you too tired after all of that snow clearing?"

"I'll clean up our dinner dishes, take a quick shower and then I'll happily beat you at Scrabble."

"Ha! Game on mister!"

He felt relieved and happy that she had asked him to stay. It was unexpected, a shock even. But he was grateful. He realized he was whistling as he stood under the shower spray, the hot water relieving the aches and knots in his sore muscles. He couldn't remember the last time he had whistled. Feelings of joy and lightheartedness had been foreign to him. Until now. Until Alyson. Just the thought of her had him hardening again. He adjusted the water to run cold until it made him gasp and his rebellious body finally responded and the overwhelming lust abated. Temporarily, he knew.

He did beat her at Scrabble, by an embarrassingly large margin. He wondered where some of the words were coming from. He astounded himself a couple of times. They sipped wine while they played and he relished the normalcy of the evening. This was probably how most couples passed an evening. Together, laughing, sharing a bottle of wine. It was a dream he didn't even realize he wanted. Dreams had always seemed fanciful and a waste of energy. Now they were coming so easily that he wasn't sure what to make of it. Was he changing or was something awakening inside of him? He couldn't help but smile at her as she playfully pouted when he slaughtered her in their rematch. She was adorable.

"It's official. You've worn me out."

"Victory is mine," he grinned, his eyes crinkling at the corners as he picked up the Scrabble tiles and started putting them away.

"I think I'd like to sleep upstairs in my own bed tonight. Stairs are still a bit tricky. Would you mind helping me?"

"Not at all." He offered her his hand and pulled her to her feet. Instead of lifting her into his arms as he usually did, he tossed her over his shoulder, making her squeal in what he hoped was surprised delight. He turned off lights as they walked through the first floor and effortlessly carried her up the stairs. He was moved again by how normal and right it felt. When they got to her room, he knelt down and helped her sit back on her bed.

Her hands lingered on his shoulders and their gazes locked. God it would be so easy to simply lean in and kiss her. What would she do? Would she push him away? Slap him? Christ. Would she kiss him back? He was pretty sure she wasn't breathing either as they stared into each other's eyes, trapped in the intensity of the moment. He wanted to kiss her. He wanted to taste her more than he'd ever wanted anything in his life. Fear prevailed though and he cleared his throat and reluctantly pulled away from her. Her hands slipped from his shoulders and she wouldn't meet his gaze as he stood.

"Do you need anything before I go?" he asked, willing her to look at him.

She glanced up quickly, "No thanks. Please take the guest room tonight."

"Thank you. I will. Good night, Alyson."

"Good night, John."

Walking out of her room was one of the hardest things he had ever done. With every fiber of his being he wanted to slip under the covers with her and hold her in his arms. He wanted to make her sigh with pleasure and lose himself in her sweetness. He knew sleep would prove elusive tonight as he wondered what might have happened had he kissed her instead of walking away.

CHAPTER 15

Alyson was relieved that her foot was strong enough to allow her to drive. They were shocked by the mountains of snow piled along the sides of the roadway as they left her house and merged onto the main thoroughfare that would take them into the city. Thanks to a cancellation, she was able to get an appointment to see her doctor at ten. Her foot was already feeling much better but she still wanted to have it checked out. The clinic was located in a strip mall and John assured her he would amuse himself while he waited for her. She gave him her extra car key and returned his wave as she hobbled the short distance to the clinic door.

Dr. Price was a slender middle-aged woman with spiky grey hair and dark brown eyes that shone with kindness and empathy. She examined the cut on Alyson's head and noted that it was healing quite well on its own and didn't require stitches. She ran a series of tests to rule out concussion. She was confident that Alyson's foot was not broken but insisted on an x-ray to confirm. Dr. Price gave her crutches to use in the meantime. When Alyson thought of how close she had come to perishing in that forest, she felt a surge of relief and gratitude that she was walking away relatively unscathed.

John wasn't in the car when she returned so she wandered into the pharmacy adjacent the clinic to purchase a few things she needed. She made her way slowly around the store adding items to the small basket she had picked up at the entry. Shopping on crutches was a little awkward but she was managing. She hadn't bothered with makeup in the last couple of years so she paused at the cosmetics counter and selected a new lipstick and mascara. She didn't want to dwell on the sudden interest in making herself more attractive, because that led back to the moment in her bedroom last night. The moment where she was certain John was about to kiss her. She had been terrified. Terrified he would close the distance and press his lips to hers. Even more terrified that he wouldn't. She had almost pulled him to her. God she had wanted to feel his lips on hers and his hands on her body. He was awakening needs and desires that she had forgotten even existed. She pulled herself back to the present, swallowing for the millionth time the disappointment that the encounter hadn't resulted in a kiss. It was for the best. She almost believed that.

She was out of her favourite body lotion so she hobbled down the aisle until she found it. She picked up an extra body wash for John and wondered if he needed other items. She'd ask him when she returned to the car. She selected a couple of magazines, one on travel and the other on photography. Maybe she'd plan a trip somewhere early next year. Maybe Europe or the Caribbean. Perhaps Lois could take time off work to go with her. She smiled to herself knowing how much that would mean to Lois. She fought hard to suppress the surge of guilt that flooded her as she realized how completely she had pushed away her family and friends, emotionally and now geographically. It was so unfair to them. She would try harder and do better.

She paid for her purchases and headed toward the car. She wondered if John would like to go out for lunch. He didn't enjoy being around people so maybe it was a bad idea to ask. She stopped just shy of her vehicle when she noticed a tall man leaning against the passenger door. Dear God he was handsome. With a rush of heat she realized it was John. His hair was cut short, not military short but almost. The beard was gone. He looked like he was holding his breath waiting for her to recognize him. When her eyes lit up in acknowledgement, a slow smile spread across his face and she was shocked by her physical reaction to him. Her knees actually felt weak. Good grief, talk about hiding your light under a bushel.

"What did your doctor say?" he anxiously asked.

Alyson quickly filled him in on the details of her visit, her gaze not straying from his face as she continued to stare at him.

"This is what you were hiding under all of that hair?" she teased.

"Am I hideous?"

"Ha! You know the answer to that!"

"Seriously. Is it okay? I feel naked."

"You are stunning. I can't stop staring."

"Then don't," he grinned, giving her a wink that stole her breath.

Her heart slammed against her ribcage. She hadn't felt attracted to anyone like this since Joe. In the months before moving here, she had gone on two blind dates just to make Syd and Lois stop bugging her. Both ended in disaster. The first guy had tried to kiss her and she screamed at him to back off. The second guy was so interested in himself that he hadn't even notice she was bored. She ended that date early and didn't look back. She also insisted that her sister and best friend stop trying to fix her up. She told them there was no one else for her but Joe.

She felt a momentary pang of disloyalty to Joe as she settled into the car next to John. Since last night she had been daydreaming of kissing this man. More than that. She had been fantasizing about being intimate with him. Joe was gone forever. She had to start living in the moment. This gorgeous man sitting next to her was her present. He wasn't necessarily her future, but he was her here and now. She felt butterflies as she pondered possibilities. She was willing to bet that her family and Lois would not approve of even a fleeting relationship with John. Knowing, or more accurately, not knowing his past and circumstances would freak them out. It still freaked her out a little but she was getting better at pushing it from her mind. It was much easier to forget everything else now that she could see his face. His jaw was square and strong, the newly exposed skin slightly paler. His jade eyes seemed even more startling against his clean-shaven face and sexy haircut. He looked like a model out of a magazine. Surely if he belonged to someone else they would have turned the world upside down to find him. She sure as hell would if he were hers.

"Alyson, are you going to start the car?" he asked, grinning at her with absolute pleasure at her discomfiture.

She grinned and cheekily replied, "Oh do shut up."

His laughter filled the car and she smiled so wide that her face hurt as they pulled into traffic.

CHAPTER 16

John was pretty sure he was the happiest man on the face of the earth. Sitting in the car next to this amazing woman, and engaging in witty repartee underscored with palatable sexual tension, was more than he ever could have dreamed possible. He felt overcome with joy and it was such a foreign feeling. The closest he had experienced in the expanse of his memory was his discovery that he could draw. But this was on a different plane. This was connecting with another soul in such a beautiful, organic way. How had he lived without this connection? Without this woman? He prayed that his memory would not fail him as it sometimes did. He wanted to imprint every nuance of this moment in his brain forever.

They stopped at a red light and she looked at him, shook her head and sighed. He chuckled at the sincerity of her appraisal and for the first time in memory, he felt good about himself. He didn't feel scary or odd or an outsider. Even having the stylist cut his hair and shave his beard had been tolerable, mildly uncomfortable yes, but he pushed through no problem. That's not something he could have done even a week ago. Not before Alyson.

When he had seen his reflection in the mirror, he felt a moment of panic. He had hoped that seeing himself clean-shaven might spark some memory, but no such luck. Perhaps he had always had a beard. He felt and looked completely different without it. His first thought had been to wonder what Alyson would think. Every thought seemed to begin and end with her. In the space of a few short days he couldn't help but wonder how he would fare moving on, leaving her behind. He resigned himself to be grateful for whatever time they carved out. It was already much more than he ever expected or felt he deserved.

They stopped at the hospital so Alyson could have her foot x-rayed. John wanted to get her a wheelchair but she didn't mind using the crutches. There weren't any other patients in the lab waiting area so she was called in almost immediately. John anxiously counted down the minutes while she was in the lab. Twenty-five minutes and thirty-three seconds passed before she emerged, the crutches in her hand.

"That looks promising," he said, expectantly.

"Not broken," she grinned. "The technician uploaded my x-rays so my doctor could review and she said I'm good to go."

"That's awesome! You still have to use the crutches?"

"When I feel I need them. It's a long trek to the car so I'll use them for now."

"I wish I had a driver's license. I'd bring it around for you."

"It's okay. It's such a beautiful day that I'm looking forward to a few minutes in the fresh air."

They returned to the car and Alyson pulled out of the hospital parking lot. Their next stop was the police station and he was nervous, scared out of his mind if he was being completely honest. What if they took one look at him and realized he was on some 'most wanted' list? He had to know but it was eating him up inside. Alyson asked him if he wanted her to come inside with him and his initial response had been to say no, but he realized he needed her for support. And he wanted her to know whatever it was that he was facing. She deserved his complete honesty. It was the only thing he had to offer her. She opted to leave her crutches in the car since the building was nearby.

She reached for his hand as they walked across the parking lot to the main entrance of the city police detachment. He squeezed her fingers in gratitude. She made some joke about the location of the donut shop next door to the headquarters building and he chuckled, happy he wasn't facing this alone. Her presence helped temper his anxiety. He could do this.

He approached the glass fronted wicket when they entered the building and asked the receptionist if there was an officer they could speak with about an unusual situation. They were told to take a seat in the waiting area and assured that someone would be with them momentarily. John hoped that was true. The longer this dragged on the more difficult it would be to find his voice. They were the only ones in the waiting area though the tiled floor was wet from the melted snow tracked in by visitors who had waited before them. After only a handful of minutes, a small-framed, balding man in his mid-fifties approached them and identified himself as Sergeant Adams and invited them to follow him into his office. It barely qualified as an office, more closet sized with a battered walnut desk, fake leather office chair and two plastic visitor's chairs crammed into the windowless space. The fluorescent lights were harsh and John could feel a headache building in this right temple.

"What can I do for you today?" Sergeant Adams asked, looking from Alyson to John.

John cleared his throat, "I, uhm, I don't really know where to start."

He looked to Alyson for reassurance and she smiled at him, nodding slightly. He returned her smile, took a deep breath and turned back toward the Sergeant who was patiently waiting.

"I don't know who I am. I've had memory lapses that have spanned ten years, perhaps more, including any knowledge of my identity, where I'm from, where I might have worked. Whether I have a family. I think I might be American. I've spent time there but I can't be sure if that's where I'm originally from."

The Sergeant leaned back in his chair, his eyebrows raised, "Now that's not something we hear every day. Have you reported this to any other police authority?"

"No sir."

"May I ask why not?"

"Honestly I was afraid of what I would find out. I feel as though I've been running from something but I have no idea what that something might be."

"Do you think your life might be in danger?"

"I honestly don't know."

"You said that you have memory lapses. Do you remember anything at all?"

"Not really, no. Sometimes I remember being on a city street but I can't tell where or when."

"Well if you can't remember anything more than that, the first thing we need to do is figure out who you are. We have our work cut out for us. Tell me about what you do remember, other places you've been and we'll start a file. Let's figure this out. Okay?"

John nodded and started answering the Sergeant's questions, relaying information he had already shared with Alyson and a few details that hadn't come up yet. He glanced at her frequently but she didn't falter, not once, always offering a kind smile and occasionally reaching out to touch his arm with a reassuring squeeze when frustration threatened to take hold. For two hours John recalled every detail and memory that he could right up to present time, including his encounter with Alyson in the forest and that he was staying with her short-term.

"Okay John. If you remember anything else, give me a call and I'll add those details to your file. Our next step is to refer you to Social Services. They will assign a caseworker to help you with housing and medical assessment. We need to figure out what is causing your memory loss."

"That sounds good," John nodded.

"I also want to send your photo to local and national media. It's our best shot at someone recognizing you and helping to identify you."

"Wow. I hadn't thought that would be a possibility," John felt panicked at the thought.

"I know it's overwhelming but we'll keep your location private and provide only minimal details. It really is our best shot at figuring out who you are."

"Okay then. You know best."

"I'd also like to fingerprint you and run it through our database. It's unlikely that you would be in the system but let's rule it out."

"Of course," John said, swallowing the bile rising in his throat. This part made him most nervous. He hoped he was running from someone bigger and scarier than him and not the law.

"I'll ensure the caseworker contacts you soon. You must be anxious to secure a place to stay."

Alyson spoke for the first time. "It's up to John, of course, but I have a huge house and he is welcome to stay with me."

"Alyson that's incredibly generous of you, but not necessary," John said, touched that she would make the offer.

"Again it's up to you, but I could really use your help for the next week or so while my foot gets stronger."

"If my staying helps you in any way, then yes, I'd be happy to stay. Thank you."

"Are you certain, Ms. Fisher?" Sergeant Adams asked.

"Yes. Absolutely. John saved my life. It's the least I can do."

Alyson and John exchanged a long look, filled with the messy, complicated feelings that were developing between them.

The Sergeant nodded. "Okay then. We will assign an investigator to your case and he or she will be in touch."

John was fingerprinted and had his photo taken, front and side profile for the media release. They provided Alyson's house and cell numbers and her street address as John's temporary contact information. Sergeant Adams promised to call if there was any news. They thanked him for his help and left the stuffy building, happy to walk back into the sunshine.

"I'm glad that's over. Thank you for sitting by me through all of that. And thank you again for asking me to stay."

"My pleasure. I guess now we wait, huh?"

"Yeah. That wheel is set in motion. It was the right thing to do."

"Yes. I believe so, too. Would you like to have lunch somewhere?" she asked. "If you'd rather not be around people, that's okay. We can go home and fix something there."

"No. I'd like to go out. It's odd but people don't bother me the same since meeting you."

She smiled at him as they got back into her car. She drove to a downtown restaurant overlooking the water, nothing fancy most likely in deference to him. John ordered a burger and fries and Alyson chose quiche and salad. The restaurant wasn't busy and they blended in seamlessly with the other patrons. He was struck again by how normal this seemed, despite being so far removed from how he had been living for at least the past decade. He wondered how long it would take the police to find something. He wondered what kind of media circus they would face once his photo was released. Hell it would probably run in American news outlets too. He had a moment of panic, wanting to remain sheltered in the security of his assured anonymity. But then he looked at Alyson, at the way the early afternoon sunlight pouring in through the window made her dark hair glow, and he knew this was the right thing to do. No matter what.

CHAPTER 17

Alyson decided to make a quick stop at the mall to replace her cell phone. She found a parking spot close to the entrance and decided to leave her crutches in the car again. John accompanied her inside.

"Do you need anything while we're here?" she asked as they walked the short distance to the telecom store.

"I do actually. Is there a pharmacy here? I have to buy a razor," he grinned.

"Yes upstairs next to the food court. The escalators are that way," she pointed to the left, squelching the impulse to touch his smooth jaw.

"I won't be long. If you finish before I return just go back to the car. Don't stay on your foot too long."

"Okay," she smiled, appreciating his concern. "Oh! I already bought you another body wash."

He looked at her with such tenderness that she felt as though he had physically touched her even though he was standing a couple of feet away from her.

"Thank you, Alyson." His voice seemed gruff and she wondered the last time someone had done something nice for this man. He waved as he walked away from her and she watched him until he glanced back and caught her. Busted. She grinned and walked into the store to look at phones.

She had been tempted to ask him if he needed money but he had insisted on paying for lunch despite her ardent protests. He had pulled several American bills from his pocket so she could only assume he had savings from his work on the fishing boat in Maine. She just hoped it wasn't the last of his savings.

She selected a phone and had it activated on her existing account. The entire process took less than ten minutes. There was no sign of John so she returned to the car to wait for him. She wondered if he would still be here by Christmas. Would they have parted ways by then? Would they see each other over the holidays? Not if he had a life waiting for him somewhere else. He approached the car a few minutes later holding a plastic bag filled with his toiletry items.

"Hi," she greeted as he sat in the passenger seat and pulled on his seatbelt. "Anywhere else you need to go?"

"Hi yourself," he smiled. "No. I'm good. I'll go wherever you want."

"Let's go home," she said, carefully navigating her car out of the busy parking lot, looking forward to spending more time alone with John.

When they returned to her house he disappeared upstairs into the spare room, presumably to put away his purchases. Alyson went into the kitchen to clean up the breakfast dishes she had insisted they leave on the counter that morning.

"You're still supposed to rest," he said, walking into the kitchen a few minutes later.

"I will. No worries. How are you feeling about everything that happened today?" she asked as they moved into the living room and sat across from each other.

"I wasn't expecting the media blitz suggestion. That definitely threw me."

"I could tell you were bothered by that."

"It's weird to think that my face will be on the front pages tomorrow."

"And television too. It's such a handsome face. I can't stop staring at you," she said, her cheeks flushing with colour at her admission.

"I'm happy you think so. And in the spirit of full disclosure, I think you're the most beautiful creature I've ever seen in my life. So there."

She smiled and their gazes held. She willed him to walk across the few feet separating them and kiss her. The shrill ringing of the telephone dashed her hopes as reality intruded.

"Let me grab the cordless for you," he offered, already halfway to the kitchen.

She smiled her thanks as he handed her the phone. "Hello," she said into the phone, her eyes never leaving John's face.

She passed him the phone, "It's for you. She said she was with Social Services."

His hand brushed hers as he took the phone and her skin tingled. Two years without intimacy suddenly seemed an unbearably long stretch of time.

"Hello. This is John," he said, his eyes not leaving Alyson's as he sat across from her. She watched his face intently while he spoke with his caseworker, appreciating his incredible bone structure and the sensual shape of his full lips as he formed words. She couldn't help draw comparisons between him and Joe. Her husband had been blond and fair complexioned. John was dark. Figuratively too. She was drawn to that, perhaps because he was so different from Joe. Perhaps because she was alone and lonely and his unexpected arrival in her world had awakened desires she'd suppressed. He was still staring at her and she wondered if he could read her thoughts. She also wondered how much of the phone conversation had actually registered with him as he disconnected the call.

"That was my caseworker," he said, his voice low, deep. "She wants to set up an appointment for ten tomorrow morning. Here, if that's okay?"

"Of course it's okay. What's her name?"

"Bernadette. I've already forgotten her last name."

"You can use the kitchen. I'll pop out so you can have privacy."

"I want you there, Alyson, if it's not too much of an imposition."

"It's no imposition. Of course I'll stay for the meeting if that's what you want."

"Thank you," he said softly, his face lighting up in the most brilliant of smiles.

Something flipped inside of her when he smiled like that. Some switch that ignited a deep-seated lust that shocked her. She didn't even want to think about it or analyze it. She simply wanted to enjoy the feelings of desire and longing and let it fuel her fantasies. John would be moving on soon. She couldn't lose sight of that. He might have a wife and family who miss him and love him and want him back. He might have committed a crime. He might be any number of things. But right now he was here, in her space, and she had to figure out what to do with that. What she was willing to risk of herself if she allowed him any closer.

The damn phone rang again and she jumped at the intrusion. John chuckled and handed it to her across the coffee table.

"Hello," she said, once again. This time it was the police. The caller identified herself as Officer Delaney and asked to speak with John.

Alyson passed the phone back to John, telling him who was on the line.

"Does your phone have a speaker function?"

"Yes. Top button on the left."

"I want you to listen."

"You're sure?"

"Yes."

John pressed the speaker button and greeted the officer.

"Mr. Smith, this is Officer Delaney. I'm working on your case with Sergeant Adams. We've run your fingerprints through CPIC and Interpol and there have been no matches. You don't have a criminal record."

"Thank God," John replied. Alyson closed her eyes in silent gratitude.

"Your photo and details have also been sent to major provincial, national and American media outlets. This time tomorrow your story will be public. We will keep you posted."

"Thank you for the update." John replied, disconnecting the call.

"You must be so relieved," she said, smiling.

"I am. I've lived with that fear for so many years," his voice broke as he rubbed his hands over his face. "Of course I might be a first time offender."

"John I can't see that. You're so thoughtful and kind and gentle. I can't imagine you hurting anyone."

"Neither can I," he whispered, his eyes full of tears.

She moved to his couch, wrapping her arms around him as he held her close and they both shed silent tears of gratitude for the first of, what would hopefully be, a long run of good news. After a couple of moments, Alyson broke the embrace but stayed next to him on the sofa. They spent the next hour talking and imaging different outcomes, all positive.

"Maybe you're some rock star who faked his own death because you couldn't handle the adoration of millions of sex crazed women."

He laughed. "Maybe I'm a reclusive millionaire disillusioned with the state of the world and chose a life of solitude as a recluse."

"That sounds too much like my story," she said softly.

"Sorry."

"Don't be sorry. I chose to hide from the world as I dealt with the pain of losing Joe."

"And now?"

"Now I want to stop living in the past and make a life for myself here. A real life."

"That sounds like a great plan. I'm happy for you."

"Thank you. It seems a little clichéd but coming so close to dying on that trail gave me a solid dose of perspective that I desperately needed."

John reached for her hand, gently holding it between both of his, stroking the inside of her wrist with his thumb. Alyson's pulse quickened and she turned her head to meet his gaze.

"Alyson," her name was half prayer, half plea on his lips as he closed the distance between them and captured her mouth with his.

She didn't resist. She didn't push him away. She plunged her hands into his cropped hair and she returned his kiss with a hunger and desperation that shocked her. He wrapped her in his arms as he deepened the kiss. A deep moan filled the silence. It was enough to break the spell. She pulled back from his lips and pressed her forehead to his, not completely severing their connection.

"Alyson, I'm sorry," he started to apologize.

"Don't you dare. That was lovely. Don't say you're sorry. I'm not. I'm just afraid of rushing into anything. There hasn't been anyone since Joe."

"It's okay. I understand. The truth is I'm not sorry. I've wanted to kiss you for days. I've dreamed of kissing you."

"Me too," she confessed.

He didn't even try to hide the smile that was splitting his face in half.

"You have an amazing smile. I love how it reaches your eyes and makes them crinkle at the corners."

"I rarely smiled until you."

John brushed her hair back from her face and gazed into her eyes. "You're beautiful," he whispered before his lips sweetly brushed against hers. He pulled away before either of them could deepen the kiss and start something they weren't ready to finish. Quite yet.

"What would you be doing if I wasn't here?" he asked, clearing his throat.

"Probably drinking wine and reading. Or hiking. Though the trails are probably too snow covered now."

"I noticed you have quite a collection of wine bottles in the garage."

"Sometimes I have to numb the pain."

"Sometimes?"

"Most days. But I haven't felt that need in the past few days. Not since you came along." She knew she was becoming too invested in him, too quickly. She just couldn't seem to help herself.

He kissed her again. A long, lingering, sweet kiss filled with promise, hinting at deeper desires. She had forgotten how much she enjoyed kissing. How sensual and erotic it was to have someone else explore your mouth, and you explore his in return. She was hit broadside by the riptide of lust that swept through her. She wanted this man. She wanted to feel that closeness with another human being again. The closeness that only came from being joined, in every way. She was a heartbeat away from making the decision to seduce him when he ended their kiss again. Dammit.

"If we don't stop now, Alyson, I'm going to be in serious trouble," he said, his eyes were filled with longing.

Thank God for him being the voice of reason. She felt torn but common sense was taking hold. He was right. They had to diffuse the moment before they were both naked on her rug.

Suppressing a moan at the though of John naked, she smiled, "We need to take a breather."

"Agreed," he said, tucking her hair behind her ear.

"I think I'll read for a while and rest my foot."

"Sounds good. Is it okay if I use your computer?" he asked. "I haven't read the news in weeks, not since leaving Maine. I used to visit the community centre most evenings there and take advantage of the free computer access. Most folks in town had their own computers so I usually had that corner of the building to myself."

"Of course! Help yourself. There isn't a password or anything."

"You're sure you don't mind?"

"Not at all. We can have leftover lasagna for dinner if that's okay?"

"That sounds amazing. Thank you."

"You're welcome," she smiled, hoping he'd kiss her before leaving the room and he did hesitate but turned and walked away as though thinking better of it. He had much more willpower than she did right now. She grabbed a bottle of fizzy water, flicked on the fireplace and got comfy on the sofa with her foot elevated. She picked up her e-reader and resumed reading the psychological thriller she had started during the storm. The book was good but her thoughts kept returning to John. And his clean-shaven face. And his soul searing kisses. She wondered what her family and friends would think of him. In addition to her mom's call, Syd and Lois had also called to check on her over the past few days as they heard about the storm but she had omitted the part about getting hurt and John staying with her. She didn't want to worry them needlessly and if she told them she had opened her home to a stranger with no memory or identity, they would definitely worry. If the situation was reversed and one of them had taken in a homeless stranger with no recollection of the past, she would probably fret too.

But they didn't know John. The realization hit her that no one knew John, not as she was getting to know him. His blank slate of a past scared her. Of course it did. But every day that passed revealed more and more of a man she genuinely liked and respected. She wanted to learn more about him. She secretly prayed that when he learned who he was that he was free and clear and that what just transpired between them wasn't some unwitting betrayal of a forgotten wife and family. She especially hoped that when they did make love, and she was pretty sure it was a foregone conclusion that they would, sooner or later, that she could guard her heart and not fall completely for him. She had honestly believed there was no one for her but Joe. Now she wasn't so sure.

CHAPTER 18

John read through the news and checked "most wanted" lists and "missing persons" directories as he did every time he sat down in front of a computer. As always, he was relieved to not see his own likeness staring back at him from the first search, though so much time had passed that it wasn't likely he'd suddenly be added to that list now. If he had committed some heinous crime or act, odds were in his favour that he had gotten away with it. Of course the police could knock on Alyson's door any moment with news to the contrary. He felt a knot in his stomach just thinking about it. Just because his fingerprints weren't in the database didn't mean he hadn't committed a crime. His thoughts flitted to Alyson and for the hundredth time he hoped that wasn't the case.

He was surprised to realize he had wiled away more than two hours in front of the screen. He hadn't heard a sound from downstairs so Alyson was either absorbed in her book or sleeping. He thought of their kisses earlier and wondered if she had any idea how close he had been to sitting back on the couch and pulling her across him so that she straddled his lap. He had no remembered experience with control. He had no point of reference, other than fictional novels, for what was acceptable in taking a relationship to the next level. He already felt so much emotion for this woman and he was terrified of something in his past destroying the trust they had built, the tenuous relationship they were forging. Their connection was fragile and could be snuffed out by any number of possible scenarios as he started down this road to self-discovery.

He reached the bottom of the stairs and saw that she had fallen asleep on the couch, the e-reader still in her hand. He walked softly towards her and took the device from her hand, placing it on the coffee table. He reached for the blanket on the back of the couch and pulled it over her. She stirred in her sleep and stretched. His body instantly reacted. She slowly blinked open her eyes and smiled up at him.

"I fell asleep?"

"Yeah you did. It's past six already."

"Oh wow," she stifled a yawn, "I didn't mean to sleep. Are you hungry?"

"Starving," he huskily replied.

"I'll heat the lasagna," she offered, pulling herself into a sitting position.

"It's not lasagna I want," he said.

"Oh. I can make something else then."

"Alyson."

The timbre of his voice drew her gaze to meet his.

"Oh," her lips formed the word but no sound escaped.

Not breaking their gaze, she pushed the blanket aside, a silent invitation for him to join her.

He groaned and hesitated for only a moment before pushing her back on the couch and stretching out over her, bearing his weight on his elbows as his mouth hungrily found hers. Their legs tangled as he settled more intimately against her. She moaned in pleasure and he fought to regain some semblance of control as the eroticism of her need filled him. He tried to reposition them on the narrow couch but almost fell off the edge.

"Bedroom," she demanded.

"You're sure?" he asked.

"Now," she commanded.

He lifted her in his arms and walked upstairs with her. He turned in the direction of the guest room and gently placed her on the edge of the bed. He stepped back and pulled off his shirt. She mirrored his actions, revealing a lacy red bra beneath the sweater she had been wearing. His hands reached out to her, tentatively cupping her breasts in his hands. He wanted to taste her. Needed to taste her. He fumbled with the hook and eye closure at the back of her bra, finally releasing it, finally removing the beautiful lingerie from her incredible breasts. She was small but full, her breasts perfectly round and tipped with large dark rose coloured areolae and thick, distended nipples. He eased her back on the bed and stretched out next to her. He may have actually whimpered he felt such a deep desire to taste her. Her back arched off the bed when he captured her nipple in his mouth and he wanted to weep with the perfection of her reaction. She was beautiful and responsive and in this moment, she belonged to him. He worshipped her breasts for several long moments, savouring the taste and feel of her. He loved how aroused and impatient she was becoming. He experienced for the first time in memory the pleasure of teasing a woman. The power and sensuality of foreplay. He was reaching for the button on her jeans when the house phone rang, the shrill tone making them both jump as they crashed back to reality.

"It might be the police," she said, pressing a kiss against his cheek before rushing to her bedroom as quickly as her injured foot would allow.

He followed just in case it was for him. She covered the receiver and said, "It's your social worker."

"Crappy timing," he grumbled as he gazed longingly at her bare breasts and reluctantly accepted the phone. Bernadette had to change their meeting time the next day by an hour. He appreciated her consideration but cursed her timing as he disconnected the phone. Alyson walked out of her closet wearing a tee shirt.

"You got dressed," he complained.

"It seemed prudent, given you were talking to your social worker."

"Prudence sucks."

She laughed at his annoyance and looped her arms around his neck as he hoisted her into his arms walked them back to the guest room.

"We could have stayed in my bedroom," she offered.

"True. But I bought condoms today and they're in this room," he grinned.

"Pretty sure of yourself, huh?" she asked, genuinely surprised.

"Not at all. But a man can dream. And lady, you make me dream."

"You're forgiven," she smiled, pulling him down on top of her onto his bed.

He kissed her for several minutes, wanting to move faster but realizing the gravity of what they were about to experience together.

"Are you sure about this, Alyson?" he asked, pushing her hair back off her forehead and tracing the curve of her cheek with his fingers.

"Yes. There hasn't been anyone since Joe. That's too long."

"Do you feel like you're being unfaithful to him, being in my arms? Kissing me?"

Surprise flitted across her face, "That's an unexpected question."

"I just think that if you were mine and I lost you for whatever reason that I couldn't be with anyone else."

"Oh John. We don't know what we're facing yet. It's fine to joke about what ifs like we were doing earlier but what if they include a wife and family?"

"I know. I think about that too. I can't understand why I wouldn't have been reported missing. Why they wouldn't have found me."

"That confuses me too," she admitted.

"I know we have to be careful. I know that we should probably wait until we know for sure who I am and what we're facing before we let ourselves fall deeper into this relationship. Is it okay if I call it a relationship?"

"I don't know what else to call it. I care about you. I care about your happiness."

"Me too. And I want to be with you. Even if there is a wife and a family, I don't know that now and I selfishly want to be with you."

"That scares me so much. Being intimate with you not knowing if you're breaking a promise to someone else."

"I don't want to break promises either. But I want you. Even if I can never have you, I want you and I want you to know that."

They stared into each other's eyes, silently letting feelings and desires tumble into place.

She reached for him first, stretching to kiss him, wrapping her legs around his hips. He hungrily kissed her back, deepening the kiss, pressing his body hard against hers.

"Please lose the shirt," he softly commanded. She pulled it over her head and tossed it to the floor. He bent to kiss each breast and then reached for her jeans, quickly releasing the button and zipper and pulling them and her panties over her hips. She was naked before him on his bed and he wondered if his heart would survive her loveliness.

"Don't move," he whispered, as he got off the bed and went into the closet to get the condoms. When he returned he tossed the box onto the bed and stood before her, quickly shedding his own clothing. She moaned at the sight of him and he was flooded with joy and hope and lust.

"Please come here," she said, reaching for him. He took a moment to roll on a condom and then lowered himself over her. He kissed her mouth and teased her with his fingers before slowly pushing inside of her, filling her, making them both moan with excitement and need. He couldn't imagine anything feeling more perfect or right than this moment. They moved together as though they had been lovers for years and when he drove her over the edge of ecstasy, he quickly followed. Okay, maybe this was the most perfect moment. Ever.

CHAPTER 19

Alyson feared her heart would beat clear out of her chest. God that had been amazing. He was still inside of her and he was holding her as though he never wanted to let go. Fine by her. Her internal muscles were still spastic and whenever they clenched around him he would moan. She loved the primal intimacy of his reluctance to vacate her body. It was doing crazy things to her head and to her heart.

"You are amazing," he said, still breathless. "You might kill me but God what a way to go."

She laughed. "You were okay I guess," she teased.

"Okay?! Okay!? Is that why I can still feel you squeezing me? Huh?" He tickled her hip.

"Don't! I'm really ticklish!"

"Then tell me it was better than okay."

"You want the truth?"

"Yes. Please," he suddenly seemed endearingly vulnerable.

"This was the best sex I've ever had. I mean that sincerely. You're very attentive and incredibly skilled. You are definitely experienced."

"Really? The best?" he asked, incredulously.

"The best," she confirmed, eyes widening as she felt him growing harder and bigger inside of her.

"Already?" she asked.

"Looks that way! Let me take care of the protection and I'll be right back." He bounded out of the guest room with a lightheartedness she had not witnessed in him before. Alyson laughed with delight. She hadn't felt this happy in a very long time.

Their second time was slower and more exploratory. He wanted to taste every inch of her and she took her time teasing every inch of him. He wasn't satisfied until she reached orgasm twice before he finally filled her again, holding her gaze with his as he gently thrust in and out of her body. It was the sweetest experience of her life.

Afterwards he held her in his arms and she asked to stay with him during the night. The joy on his face was palpable and she was pretty sure it mirrored her own. They talked long into the night, making love one more time before falling into a deep sleep. She wanted this dream to go on forever. She wanted to ask him to run away with her and disappear so that they didn't have to worry about what tomorrow might bring. About who he might be and what or who might be waiting for him at the end of a decade long disengagement. She forced herself to ignore the selfishness of her thoughts and took comfort in the safety of his arms, not stirring until the morning sun streamed in through the window. They had forgotten to close the drapes last night.

He was still sleeping and she took advantage of the quiet moment to watch him. His face was shadowed with whiskers and he looked roguishly handsome. His lips were beautifully shaped, as though sculpted and it took every ounce of strength she had not to lean forward and kiss him. His jaw was square and masculine, reflecting his strength and perseverance. The muscles in his arms were well defined as though he worked out but she knew they were the result of physical labour and survival. His chest was completely hairless and there was something especially sexy about that.

She stretched a little, testing her muscles after their incredible workout the night before. She felt sore but every ache was worth it. She loved the way he was still holding her. Even in his sleep he wanted to keep her close. She melted at that thought. A few days ago she couldn't imagine ever being close to another man again. She had walls that she believed weren't scalable and a fortress around her heart that felt impenetrable. She knew part of her connection to him stemmed from gratitude for saving her life. She also knew it went deeper than that. She had fallen in love with Joe quickly and some elemental part of her knew that she was on the same track with John. She wouldn't survive a second heartbreak. She was certain of that. But she could no more turn him away than live without breathing.

"If this is a dream please, please, please don't wake me," he said, pulling her tightly against him and kissing her forehead.

"Don't wake me either," she sighed, wrapping around him.

"How much time do we have until the social worker arrives?" he asked, already hard against her.

"Enough," she moaned as his hands slipped under the covers and pushed her legs wide open.

"Good," he whispered and she shuddered at the promise of so much pleasure wrapped up in one tiny word.

CHAPTER 20

The caseworker was a stunning woman with beautiful caramel skin and black corkscrew curls that were riotously escaping from the clip that attempted to hold them back in some semblance of order. Her name was Bernadette Pierce but she insisted they call her Bernie. She emanated a bright, beautiful energy that was infectious. John felt instantly at ease with her. He insisted that Alyson join them during their meeting. They sat around the dining room table and Alyson set out coffee and the muffins she had hastily baked after their second round of love making that morning. God she was amazing in every way. He beamed at her and only forced his attention back to Bernie after she had asked him a direct question.

He recounted his story to her and she stared at him in wide-eyed disbelief, jotting down notes and asking for more details here and there.

"This is incredible, John. Perhaps the most incredible circumstances I've ever encountered in my ten years as a social worker. There are several things we can do to help. We can set you up with temporary housing, either a room in a boarding house or a small apartment, completely your choice."

"He is welcome to stay with me as long as he needs," Alyson offered.

Bernie looked from Alyson to John, the surprise on her face was almost comical.

"Really? You're okay with that John?"

He smiled at Alyson and said, "Yes. If it's okay with Alyson I'd like to stay and help her out. She injured her foot in the storm and she doesn't have anyone else in the area. We've been helping each other." He grinned at the blush that spread across Alyson's beautiful face. She was probably thinking about the ways they had been helping themselves to each other an hour ago. He certainly was. He gave her a quick wink and returned his attention to Bernie.

"Okay. If anything changes, let me know. We have emergency housing options that I can access on short notice."

"Thank you," he said.

"I can also set you up with social assistance. It will help cover basic living expenses until we figure out who you are and where you're from."

"I don't need social assistance. I've saved a little from my last job and it should get me through the next few weeks or however long this takes."

"Okay, please let me know if your financial situation changes and I'll see what I can do to help."

"Yes ma'am, thank you."

"Since you are experiencing some sort of memory loss, I've arranged an appointment with a local GP and he will perform an initial assessment and refer you to specialists for further testing. We want to figure out what's causing your lapse in memory, whether physical or psychological. Here are the details of the appointment. Do you need me to arrange a ride for you?"

John reviewed the paper Bernie passed him. The appointment was for the next morning at nine.

"I can give John a ride to his appointment and any follow up appointments."

Bernie smiled and handed John her business card, "If Alyson is unable to drive you for whatever reason, please contact me and I will arrange a ride."

John felt incredibly grateful and hopeful. He would finally see a doctor. He could finally start working on the mystery of why he had forgotten his past. He might finally become reacquainted with the man in the mirror.

"Thank you, Bernie. I appreciate all of this so much."

"You're welcome, John. I'm hoping for a happy outcome for you." She paused for a moment and then added, "I think you should reconsider moving to St. John's. If no one recognizes you from the media appeal, this process might take weeks, maybe months. It will be a strain on Alyson to get you to and from appointments and meetings. If you were in the city you'd have access to public transit and it might be more convenient for you both."

"We'll discuss that," Alyson said, rather dismissively. John was concerned though. That would be quite an inconvenience to Alyson to have to chauffeur him around. He refused to be a burden to her. They would undoubtedly talk about that after Bernie left.

"Do you have any more questions, John?" Bernie asked as she shoved his file back in her messenger bag.

"No, but I do have your number. And thank you again." They walked Bernie out and waved goodbye from the doorway.

As soon as Bernie pulled away, Alyson closed the door and pushed John back against it, pressing against him from shoulder to hip.

"Oh there is a God and he answers prayers," John smiled, wrapping her in his arms.

"I don't want you to leave," she said, looking up at him with those bewitching blue eyes.

"Aly, it would be so much easier on you if I did."

"Easier how?" she asked, incredulously.

"Driving me to and from the city is going to be a pain in the ass for you. Plus we don't really know how long I'll be here, in the province I mean. Depending on what the police find, or don't find, my stay might be indefinite."

"You're saying you want to leave then?" Alyson asked, pulling out of his arms.

"No. That's not what I'm saying but I'm trying to be realistic. We don't know what happens next."

"That scares me."

"It scares me too. But realistically, we both know I can't stay here forever. Right?"

Alyson nodded but she didn't meet his eyes. He reached out to her but she stepped back.

"I can't right now," she whispered, her voice shaking. "I have some errands to run. "Do you want to come with me or stay here?"

"I'll stay here if that's okay."

"Of course," she said, already walking away.

Shit. She was pissed with him. He was already fucking this up and he didn't know what to do about it. He didn't want to promise her that he would stay when he honestly didn't know if he could keep that promise. The police could come and arrest him at any moment. A forgotten family could show up and claim him. A hitman could finish the job and take him out when he least expected. Fuck he could be returned to the mother ship for all he knew.

They were getting emotionally entangled, quickly. Perhaps too quickly. He didn't want to stop his relationship with Alyson, though part of him knew proceeding was probably the worse thing they could do. They both stood to get deeply hurt if they weren't careful. Who was he kidding! Not being able to see her or be with her would already cut to the quick.

She left the house a few minutes later looking young and pretty in a light grey poncho and sexy knee high boots. He melted at the sight of her. *He was falling for her. Hard.* She didn't hug him or kiss him goodbye and he felt sad, even as he understood the reason for her distance. He stood in the door as she drove away but she didn't look back. He couldn't help but wonder if they would ever get back to that incredibly intimate place they had been just a couple of short hours ago. He hoped she didn't regret sleeping with him.

He felt lost when she left and wondered what to do until she returned. He poked around in the freezer and took out a couple of steaks to thaw for their dinner. He figured he might as well read the news and see if he had made the local papers. He brewed himself a cup of coffee and went upstairs to Alyson's study, settling in at her desk. When he booted up the laptop, he was shocked to see his own face staring back at him from virtually every news site he checked. He knew it was coming but his story was making headlines everywhere.

Fuck! This was a media blitz. And it would undoubtedly work unless he had changed quite a bit in the past decade. They had kept the story pretty lean and made no mention of Alyson. Good. He didn't want to drag her into this if at all possible. He was terrified of what it would uncover. He moved restlessly to the guest room and dug his sketchbook out of his pack. Maybe drawing would calm him. It usually did. He realized it had been several days since he had sketched anything, some kind of record for him since discovering his hidden talent. He went to the living room and settled on the couch and let the pencil work its magic. He wasn't surprised to see Alyson's face emerge from the blank page. He wished he had coloured pencils to see if he could accurately capture the blue of her eyes. Her beautiful, mesmerizing eyes. Eyes that saw into the depths of his soul and heart and accepted him for who he was, or at least the parts that still existed.

She returned after a couple of hours, toting in shopping bags and tossing the daily newspaper on the kitchen island.

She dropped the bags and walked to him, and when he extended his arms, she fell into his embrace.

"I'm sorry," they both said and then smiled at each other.

"I missed you," John said, tucking her hair behind her ears and leaning down to kiss her.

"I missed you, too," she said, returning his kiss. "You made the front page of the paper."

"Yeah. I scanned the media outlets online. It's weird seeing myself everywhere."

"Now we wait."

"Yes. We're getting good at that."

"What do you have there?" she asked nodding to the sketchbook on the sofa.

"Just some doodles," he deferred.

"You draw? May I see?"

"Sure," he said, reaching for the book and handing it to her. He had never shared his drawings with anyone before and felt a little nervous at the thought of her seeing them.

"Oh my God, John. These are incredible!" she said, sinking to the sofa and slowly looking at each and every page.

He smiled but remained silent through her running commentary. He was anxiously waiting until she reached the last page and saw the sketch of her he was working on.

"Wow," she said as she finally turned a page to discover her own eyes looking back at her.

"I can't do you justice. You're too beautiful."

"You did this from memory?"

"Yes."

"John, you've captured the shape of my nose and eyes and mouth perfectly. I'm amazed."

"It's just doodling. Really."

"I don't think you appreciate how talented you are. How long have you been drawing?"

"A couple of years."

Alyson had started working her way back through the sketches again. "Any of these could be framed and hung on a gallery wall. It's incredible the detail you've achieved with just a pencil. I'm blown away."

"Thanks but you're being overly kind. They're nothing special."

"You're wrong. These are outstanding. You continuously surprise me. Thank you for allowing me to see them."

"My pleasure, " he said, accepting the book as she handed it back to him, thrilled that she was touched by his creations.

She smiled. "I bought you some things."

"You bought me things?" he asked, surprised.

"Yeah. I hope that's okay. You have so many appointments coming up that I thought you might like to have some new things. I peeked at your sizes so I hope they fit." She reached into the bags and pulled out navy blue chinos, a pale blue button down shirt and a box containing a pair of boots much dressier than his beat up hiking boots. She also had several pairs of boxers, socks, a pair of jeans and a couple of long sleeved tee-shirts. Finally she removed a black wool jacket. Definitely the dressiest thing he had ever owned.

"This is too much."

"I really wanted to do this for you."

These are the nicest clothes I've ever owned," he smiled. "Thank you. I can pay you though."

"They're a gift. Please."

"Well, thank you," he said, hugging her to him.

"My pleasure," she smiled.

"I'm happy we're not fighting any more," he said, kissing her.

"Me too. Let's go have make-up sex," she grinned, her eyes sparkling with anticipation.

"Hell yeah," he laughed, tossing her over his shoulder and taking the stairs two at a time.

CHAPTER 21

John's doctor's appointment the next morning was the first in a long string of appointments and medical testing over the next several days. John had asked Alyson if she would be present for most of it. She wondered if it was the moral support he needed or a second set of ears in case his memory started failing him again. In any case she stood by him and listened attentively to all of the medical professionals they interacted with. His case was obviously given priority status because the wait time between appointments was minimal and some of the testing had even taken place over the weekend.

Preliminary testing and reports didn't uncover any obvious physical cause for his memory loss. There was no apparent tumour or head trauma. John's final appointment on Monday afternoon was with a psychiatrist. Dr. Tucker was a tall, heavy-set man with a deep yet soft voice and a kind demeanor. He reluctantly allowed Alyson to sit in on the session. He asked John to recount his most distant memories. When John couldn't zone in on a clear memory prior to the previously recounted baseball game, Dr. Tucker started asking more direct questions about where he grew up, his family, his school, none of which John could answer.

"John since there doesn't appear to be a physical cause for your amnesia, it's most likely due to some psychological trauma."

"So what do we do next?" John asked, wondering what was in store in the days and weeks ahead.

"I'd like to continue working with you to see if I can help you unlock some of your forgotten memories. It's possible you might never recall memories from your past. That's rare but does happen sometimes."

"Okay. When do we start?"

"Book an appointment with my receptionist for early next week, whichever day works best for you. I'll fit you in."

"Thank you, Dr. Tucker," John and Alyson shook his hand and returned to the reception area. John booked an appointment for Tuesday afternoon and they left the doctor's clinic.

As they walked to the car, Alyson said, "There's a Greek restaurant nearby. Are you hungry?"

"Famished," he said, opening her car door for her.

They were talking quietly a few minutes later as they walked into the restaurant, not paying attention to the other patrons. The hostess seated them near the back of the restaurant and gave them menus. They were both absorbed in the menu offering, John absently stroking the palm of her hand, when a waitress approached their table. She was an attractive woman in her early twenties and chatted easily with them as she filled their water glasses. She started to tell them about the daily specials when she stopped mid-word.

"Oh my God. You're the guy from the news. The one who can't remember his past."

"Sorry, why does that matter?" John asked, glancing at Alyson.

"I just can't believe you're sitting here. You're bit of a celebrity around town today," she said, beaming at John.

"I'm no celebrity," John said, "May we order please?"

"Of course," she replied, giving Alyson a curious glance and noticing John holding her hand.

They placed their order and the waitress walked back to her station, excitedly talking to two of the other waitresses and nodding in their direction.

"Oh boy," John said, noticing that they were all looking their way now.

Alyson glanced over her shoulder at their unwanted audience and noticed it included more than the staff. A group of women at the table across from them also recognized John and were staring. They quickly returned their attention to their food though when they realized that Alyson was glaring at them.

"Do you want to leave?" she asked.

"No. Absolutely not. They're harmless. Let's just eat."

The rest of their dinner passed without incident and they were relieved that the waitress hadn't made any further mention of John's story in the news. However, as they opened the door to leave the restaurant, they were bombarded by at least a dozen people including media, snapping their picture and asking them about John's past and if Alyson would provide her name. John wrapped his arm around Alyson and they pushed through the crowd and hurriedly got into her car.

"That was insane," Alyson said, quickly leaving the parking lot.

"Let's drive around for a while," John suggested, "make sure no one follows us home."

"They have the make and model of my car and if they managed to get the plate number, they'll probably be able to track me down anyway."

"I'm so sorry for getting you mixed up in this," he said, reaching across to squeeze her knee.

"This isn't your fault. Someone inside the restaurant must have called the media. I'm pretty sure I heard someone offer to marry you!"

"Oh God what have I done?" John closed his eyes and tipped his head back against the headrest.

"You did the only thing you could. The attention sucks but it's your best shot at figuring out what happened to you."

"I know. I just hate that it is intruding on the lovely bubble we've been hiding in all week."

"I don't think anyone is following us. Let's go home."

They both kept anxious watch of the surrounding traffic but it seemed they were in the clear. They exited the city and headed for Alyson's country retreat, parking the car in the garage as soon as they arrived home.

They were just kicking off their boots in the mudroom when Alyson's house line rang. She went to the kitchen and picked up, mouthing to John that it was her sister.

"Alyson what the hell is going on there?"

"Syd what's wrong?"

"My friend Julie just sent me a photo of you that was taken with some mystery man who can't remember who he is or something. She said the photo was plastered all over social media. Julia recognized you immediately. Are you okay?"

"You've got to be kidding. Send me the picture."

Alyson dug her cell phone out of her purse and waited for Sydney's text to come through.

"That didn't take long," Alyson muttered as she opened the photo and realized it had been snapped from inside of the restaurant just after they ordered. Given the angle, it had most likely been captured by the women at the next table. The look on John's face in the photo as he held her hand and gazed at her could only be described as adoration. Well fuck. The media would have a field day with this. Shit.

"Everything okay?" John asked.

Alyson showed him her phone while turning her attention back to her sister, "Syd! Yes, he's here with me. Calm down. Have Mom and Dad seen this yet?"

"Sorry," John mouthed, backing out of the room.

"It's okay," Alyson mouthed back. "Syd he's not a mass murderer." She rolled her eyes at John.

"Because he doesn't have a record. The police ran his prints. It's okay."

Alyson poured herself a glass of wine though she was tempted to drink directly from the bottle.

She spent the better part of an hour talking to Syd trying to allay her fears, even admitting that she was scared of what they would find out as well. Before she hung up talking to Syd, a call from Lois came in on her cell phone. Alyson said goodbye to Sydney and answered her cell.

"Hey Lois, what's up?"

"Aly, are you okay? Syd just texted me a photo of you and some stranger and said your life might be in danger. What the hell girlfriend?"

"I am going to kill Syd," Alyson groaned. She went through the same discussion again, making the same reassurance to Lois. She finally hung up and taking a deep breath, called her parents before Sydney could get to them too. They were upset she hadn't told them about her ordeal in the woods and John's role in her rescue. For the third time in less than two hours she gave them the same spiel she had given Syd and Lois. She was emotionally drained.

She placed her cell phone on the table and looked up to see John standing in the doorway with his pack.

"What's going on?" she asked.

"I called Bernie and asked her to arrange for housing. I can't put you through this."

"John, no! It's okay, honestly."

"I heard you tell your family you were scared."

"I am scared. You know that."

"I know. Me too. But I don't want the media hounding you. I don't want to cause problems with your family. I don't want you hurt by my situation."

"The media are probably going to hound me anyway. I've already handled my family. I want you to stay."

"I want to stay but this is for the best. I have to do what's best for you," he said, his voice husky with emotion.

The doorbell rang and Alyson couldn't bear to answer it.

"I have to go," he whispered.

She nodded but didn't move.

"Thank you for everything," he said.

"Thank you," she said, her voice breaking as she launched herself into his arms.

The bell rang again. John pressed a kiss against her forehead, pulled away and gave her a sad wave as he opened the door and disappeared into the night. Her heart shattered with the soft click of the door as it closed behind him.

CHAPTER 22

The small studio apartment in a downtown building was rather shabby compared to Alyson's beautiful home, but it was the first place John had that was completely his own. Bernie had picked him up the evening before and brought him to the modestly furnished apartment located above a travel agent's office. When she told him the rental rate per month he accepted, knowing he could afford to stay here for several months if necessary.

He felt sad not waking up wrapped around Alyson. It was for the best but it still ripped his heart out. He had left three hundred dollars on the dresser in the spare room to cover the cost of the clothes she had bought for him. He had no idea if that was enough, as all of his clothes typically came from thrift stores, but he hoped it came close. He didn't feel right accepting them as gifts, as she had intended. He knew that would probably piss her off, but hey, he was on a roll.

Bernie said that she would contact the police and let them know of his change of address. She also left the number for a local phone company suggesting he'd have a landline installed. He'd never had a phone before and he was leaning more toward the convenience of a cell phone. It felt like such an extravagance but really it had become a necessity given the circumstances. It would make it easier to stay in touch with the police about his case. It would also be incredibly tempting to contact Alyson.

He picked up the map of bus routes Bernie had left him and noted there was a bus stop a couple of blocks from his new place. He needed a few things for his apartment so he pulled on a cap and dark glasses, hoping no one would recognize him. The last thing he wanted was a repeat of the restaurant scene from the evening before. He couldn't bring himself to wear the wool coat that Alyson had bought him and shrugged on his old army jacket instead. At least it was clean and made him look less like a bum. He did slip his feet into the new boots though. They were comfortable and she had nailed the sizing. He had left the old ones at her place along with the pink laces. He rode the bus to the mall and returned to the telecom store where Alyson had purchased her replacement phone. He chose a basic pre-paid phone and just like that he was connected to the outside world.

He looked at the phone in his hand and desperately wanted to call Alyson. How was it possible that he missed her so deeply when he hadn't even been away from her for twenty-four hours yet? But God he did miss her; her laughter, her smile, her kisses, her passion. He missed all of her. He longed to hear her voice. It would be so easy to call her right now. He could even remember her numbers from the meeting with the police. Funny that he couldn't remember his own name but if he heard a number once it became permanently embedded in his memory. He was a freak of nature.

He resisted the urge to call her, forcing himself to remember why he had left in the first place. He walked through the mall, absently purchasing the items he needed to make his place more comfortable and functional; towels, sheets, pillows and a comforter. He also returned to the pharmacy and picked up toiletry items he needed. He hated malls. They were filled with too many people who might recognize him. He walked outside and waited for the next bus to downtown. The bus ride took twenty-five minutes with at least ten stops but he enjoyed it. The route cut through several residential areas and it was mildly entertaining to glimpse people's lives through their windows as the bus lumbered along. His first glimpse of Alyson had been through her window. He sighed.

He let himself into his apartment, and placed his purchases on the kitchen counter. He rolled up the sleeping bag that he had slept in last night and made his bed with the new sheets and comforter. The pillows he had bought were cheap but they would do. He removed the tags from the towels and placed them on a shelf in the small bathroom. He stored his toiletry products in the narrow cabinet beneath the bathroom sink. He returned to the main room and glanced at the gaudy teal plastic clock that hung on the wall and was disheartened to realize it was only a few minutes past eleven. He had to find something to do to pass the time.

He remembered noticing a small market a couple of blocks away so he locked up his apartment and headed there to buy food. The supermarket was well stocked and even had a modest selection of small kitchen appliances. He picked up the cheapest coffee maker they had and was giddy at the thought of brewing his own coffee every morning. He lugged the bags back to his place and stored the food in the fridge and cupboards. He had even splurged on oranges and fresh milk. He set up his coffee maker, anxious to try it out. It wasn't as fancy as Alyson's single server but it would adequately feed his caffeine addiction.

Less than an hour had passed. He was going to go out of his mind. He stared out the window at the rush of humanity passing by one story down. Everyone seemed to be in such a hurry. Places to go. People to see. *If he called, would she visit him*, he wondered.

He looked around the small apartment. It really wasn't much and was minimally furnished. The single bed was pushed along the far wall and a small, roughly hewn table with a shelf served as a nightstand. There was an apartment sized couch on the opposite wall upholstered in an ugly tweed and it was the most uncomfortable piece of furniture he had ever sat on, but it was marginally better than the hard floor. A small round table with a faded Formica top was placed in front of the lone window between the bed and couch and was bracketed by two cheap, olive green vinyl covered chairs. The kitchen was u-shaped with top and bottom cabinets painted a startling shade of bright yellow. The dark brown counter tops were badly scratched in places. He was thankful for the working fridge and stove. It wasn't extravagant but it was more than sufficient to meet his needs. There were two doors on the opposite wall from the kitchen; one led to the small bathroom with basic sink, toilet and tub and the other was a walk in closet and storage room combined. It was more space than he had ever had. If he couldn't be with Alyson, this would do just fine.

He wondered what she'd think of it. He wondered if she was upset with him for leaving. He took a long swallow of coffee, as though for courage, and picked up his phone. Before he could change his mind he keyed in her cell number and hit the dial button. It rang three times before she finally picked up, sounding breathless. Even with miles between them, her breathy hello stirred his flesh and made him ache for her.

"Hello, Alyson," he said, softly.

"John! Hello. How are you?" She didn't sound upset. He felt some of the tension ease out of his shoulders.

"I'm okay. How are you?"

"I'm okay, thank you."

"I'm happy to hear that."

His words were met with a long stretch of silence. He closed his eyes, not wanting to break the connection but not sure if she wanted to talk to him either.

"It's good to hear your voice," she said so softly he almost missed it.

"I miss you," he said.

"I miss you, too. Where are you?"

"I'm in a small apartment downtown."

"Do you like it?"

"It's okay. Is it wrong that I want to see you?"

"No. I want to see you too but after last night I didn't think you'd be contacting me again."

"I'm sorry about that. I heard the grief that your family was giving you on the phone and I thought the best thing I could do for you was to leave you alone. Not complicate your life. And Jesus, look at me. I didn't even make it a day without contacting you."

"Maybe I like complications."

"Do you want to see my place?"

"Yes, I do. May I drop by?"

John gave her directions and she promised she'd see him soon. He hung up and hastily tidied the room, not that there was much to put away. He made a quick trip back to the market to pick up her favourite tea and splurged on cupcakes and biscotti. He had no idea if she liked either but he wanted to have something nice to offer her. He bought a new mug, just for her. The rest of his dishes were mismatched pieces that came with the apartment, but he wanted something unchipped and worthy of Alyson. He wanted to give her the best of everything. He laughed at the irony. He was a man with no name, no past and virtually no money and the best he could offer her was store bought baked goods. And a mug without cracks.

He returned to his apartment and washed the mug, thinking the cornflower blue ceramic was almost the same colour as her eyes. He filled the kettle and placed it on a burner to heat. He brushed his teeth and changed his shirt. She still hadn't arrived. He walked to the window and looked down at the street below but there was no sign of her. He was starting to fear that she had changed her mind. He walked from the window to the kitchen and back again, a distance of no more than twenty feet. Back and forth he paced, growing increasingly anxious with each moment that passed. The knock on his apartment door a few moments later made him jump. He wiped his sweaty palms on his jeans and walked to the door, his heart pounding. When he pulled it open, she was standing there, looking like the loveliest creature he had ever seen, and she was holding two large reusable shopping bags.

"Hi," he said, stepping aside so she could enter his place.

"Hi," she replied, looking around. "This is nice. Your own space. You must be pleased."

"Yeah. It's good. I'm so happy you came."

"Me too." She held out the bags, "These are for you. A few pre-cooked meals from the deli."

"You didn't have to do that."

"I know. I wanted to though. Consider it a housewarming gift."

"Thank you, Alyson." He took the bags from her and crammed the meals into the small freezer compartment of his apartment-sized fridge. He would be willing to bet there was a least three hundred dollars worth of food here, the same amount he had left in his room at the house to cover the cost of the clothing. Clever woman.

"So, this is your place," she said, standing awkwardly in the middle of his space.

"Please sit. I bought your favourite tea. Would you like some?"

"Yes please. I'd love a cup."

"Have reporters tracked you down?"

"It's only been a few hours, but honestly, I think my identity is perhaps a non-story."

"I hope you're right. Are you managing at the house okay? Are you spending too much time on your feet?" he asked as he fussed about the kitchen, reheating the water and setting the sweets on his least chipped plate.

"I'm managing just fine, I promise. So no news yet I guess?"

"No. So far no one has come forward."

"Has anyone recognized you today?"

"No. But the couple of times I went out I wore a cap and dark glasses and believe it or not, it seems to be working."

"I've noticed you didn't shave either."

"Yeah. Part of my disguise," he grinned placing her tea and the sweets on the small table.

"I love biscotti. These look great."

They made small talk while they sipped their tea but John felt sad at the awkwardness between them now. Their conversation felt forced and their eye contact was infrequent and fleeting. He didn't regret inviting her here; he had to see her. But he felt pained by the shift in their connection. And he was dying to touch her. Hug her. Kiss her. Smell her hair. He didn't have any right to do any of those things.

"Have you thought about what you'll do if no one recognizes you and your memory doesn't return?"

"Not really. I guess I need to discuss my options with Bernie. See if I can get some form of identification. I need to exist on paper to do virtually anything."

"Funny how we take that for granted."

"Yeah."

"I should probably get going. You must have stuff to do."

"You're welcome to stay as long as you want. I've missed you."

"I've missed you too." She smiled at him and their eyes held for a long moment. John was afraid to breathe.

"I really should go," she said, standing and bringing her mug to the kitchen. "Thank you for the tea and treats."

She paused at the counter, her back turned to him. He walked up behind her, stopping just shy of touching her.

"Alyson," he didn't mean for his voice to sound quite so tortured. When she didn't move away he slowly wrapped his arms around her, gently but firmly pulling her back against his front.

"John," she whispered.

"Is it okay if I do this?" he asked, his voice also a whisper, though husky.

"Yes," she said breathlessly, leaning back against him.

"Is it okay if I do this?" he asked, turning her in his arms.

"Yes," she sighed, her eyes filled with emotion.

"Is it okay if I do this?" he asked as he lowered his head and stopped just shy of kissing her.

"God yes," she murmured, stretching to close the space between their lips.

He paused and pulled back, smiling at her.

"You're sure?" he asked.

She nodded, "Please."

One of his arms remained firmly circled around her waist and his other hand moved to softly stroke her jaw line, finding a resting place tangled in the hair at the nape of her neck. He gazed into her eyes as he slowly lowered his head. His lips claimed hers with a gentleness he didn't think he was capable of given how deeply he ached for her and how completely he wanted to posses her. After a long, sweet moment, his teeth nipped at her bottom lip and when she gasped against his mouth, he deepened the kiss, his tongue lightly exploring. When he pulled back she was grasping his shirt as though holding on for dear life. He smiled and brushed his lips against her mouth again and then rested his forehead against hers.

"I could do that forever," he said, his voice deep and husky. He pulled her hard against him so she could feel his arousal pressing against her hip. He was running his hands beneath the hem of her sweater, caressing the impossibly soft skin at the small of her back, when a knock on the door penetrated the Alyson-induced haze that engulfed him.

"That's the door," she whispered, her eyes wide and cheeks flushed. He grinned at her alarm, as though they had both been caught with their hands in the cookie jar.

"I have no idea who that could be," he said, reluctantly releasing her to open the door. He was surprised to see Sergeant Adams, Bernie and an incredibly beautiful woman on his doorstep.

"Hello John," Sergeant Adams said, "May we come in? This woman came by the station late this afternoon claiming to know you. I called Bernie and we thought you'd appreciate meeting with her here in your apartment instead of doing this at the station."

John was rooted to the spot. He couldn't move. He couldn't stop staring at the woman. His reached for the doorframe, to brace himself. He could hear Alyson's voice from far away asking him if he was okay. He was pretty sure he was going to pass out. Everything was muddled. Voices. Faces. Images. Flashing in his head until it ached. Until the roar in his ears threatened to deafen him. The only thing to pierce the confusion was her voice, the stranger. Saying his name. But she didn't call him John. She called him Tate.

And she wasn't a stranger. She was his wife.

CHAPTER 23

Alyson stood in some form of suspended animation watching everything unfold. John looked as though he was having a heart attack. Everyone was saying his name. Except the stranger. She called him something else. She called him Tate. And when she did his face went white. Bernie and Sergeant Adams stepped forward to catch him before he slumped to the ground.

"Should I call an ambulance?" Alyson asked, fumbling in her purse for her phone. She wanted to rush to his side but she restrained herself even though it was killing her.

"Give him a minute. I think he's coming around," Sergeant Adams said. "Perhaps get him a glass of water."

Alyson rushed to the sink and hastily filled a glass, returning to the small entryway.

John was sitting with his back against the wall. Colour was returning to his cheeks. He was still staring at the woman. She was crying. No, that was an understatement. She was sobbing, hysterically.

"We thought you had died," she said, over and over.

"No," he said. "I didn't go into the building."

"What building?" Bernie asked.

"The World Trade Centre," John said. "On September 11, 2001. I had a meeting but I didn't go in. I was late."

There was a collective gasp around the room.

"I was on the phone with you," he said, looking at the stranger, "we were fighting. I looked up and I saw the plane fly into the north tower. I saw it. I saw it. And then I saw people jumping out of the building. Oh my god. They were just jumping."

Alyson felt tears sliding down her cheeks. This is what the poor man, John or Tate, or whatever his real name was, had witnessed. No wonder his mind had shut down. She wanted to comfort him but she was feeling very much like an outsider. Obviously this woman was from his past and perhaps she should just leave and let them sort everything out.

John had pulled himself to his feet and invited everyone inside.

"I'm actually going to leave," she said to him softly, "you obviously have much to talk about with this woman."

"I do. She's my wife, Alyson. My name is Tate Sampson, I'm an architect from New York City and this is my wife, Vicki." His voice sounded mechanical and he looked shell-shocked.

Alyson couldn't speak. This was her worst fear and fondest wish all coming to fruition. She wanted him to remember who he was and she wanted the memories to be good. She had prayed there would be no wife. But there was. Oh God. She had to get out of here. She couldn't add to the complexity of this situation for John. Tate.

She said a general goodbye to everyone in the room and left, clutching the rail as she blindly made her way down the steep flight of stairs, not letting the sobs escape until she hit the street. She truly was happy for Tate. He deserved to have his life back. But she was devastated for herself; she could have possibly loved this man. Fuck. Who was she kidding? She was already in love with this man and she couldn't have him. She rushed to her car and sat inside sobbing until she cried herself dry. She was exhausted. She somehow drove home and opened her favourite red wine. She slumped on the couch, letting the memories of her time with Joe and her time with John break her heart all over again. She drank and cried and remembered while she waited for the wine to numb her.

CHAPTER 24

Tate felt like he had fallen down the rabbit hole and was tumbling through a kaleidoscope of memories. There were snippets of conversations, images flashed in his mind making him dizzy with the strobe-light effect of the sudden onslaught of remembered experiences. Vicki. *His wife.* He had forgotten her. Looking at her, he wondered how that was possible. He remembered she had been pregnant. They had been so excited. But she had lost the baby, late term. It had crushed both of them, but especially her. He couldn't remember any other pregnancies. Any other children. He was pretty certain it had just been the two of them. They had been living in a flashy condo in NYC. He could remember minimalistic furniture with sleek, clean lines. And white. Virtually everything had been white. It felt cold and sterile now in his memory compared to the warmth of Alyson's house.

He had been an architect. It made sense given his love of drawing. He could suddenly remember building codes and slope ratios like they had never been forgotten. He designed houses. He had lived in a condo but designed houses. Energy efficient houses. Houses he remembered he wished he could live in. Houses with happy families. Happy memories. Happily ever afters.

His parents. He remembered them. He could see them as clearly in his memories as if they were standing before him.

They were fifteen years older now. That seemed incomprehensible. They would seem so much older than he remembered them. My God. So much to soak in. So much to come to terms with. His head started to pound.

He looked at Vicki. "You didn't try to find me?"

"Oh Tate. I thought you had died. I knew that you had that meeting and we had been talking on the phone and you suddenly disappeared off the line. Moments later I could hear people screaming and crying and it sounded like total chaos. Of course I had no idea what was happening until the news broke. When you didn't come home or contact me, I assumed you had been inside the building. You just disappeared and I assumed you had perished in the terrorist attack. It was devastating."

"Mom and Dad. Are they okay?"

Vicki started to cry again. "Your mom passed away eleven years ago. She had breast cancer. She fought so hard but it metastasized in her brain. It was aggressive and she died within months. Losing her so soon after losing you nearly killed your dad."

Tate started to cry, grieving the mother he had remembered and lost in the same moment. "And Dad? How is he now?"

"Oh Tate, I don't know how to tell you this."

"Oh God. Is he gone too?"

"No. But he has advanced Alzheimer's. He doesn't know anyone. He's in a nursing home in New York."

Tate put his head in his hands and let the sobs of loss and grief rip through him. His dad wouldn't even know him. That killed him. He took a deep breath and fought to pull himself together. He would go see him as soon as possible. He remembered all of their shared memories now. He'd remember for both of them.

Bernie's voice broke through the emotional overload that threatened to consume him.

"I'm so sorry for your loss, John. Sorry, I mean Tate. Sergeant Adams and I are going to leave now and let you and Vicki catch up. We'd both like to touch base with you tomorrow. I'd like to get you in to see Dr. Tucker if possible. He will be very interested in speaking with you now that your memories are returning. I can try to book an emergency appointment this evening if you'd like?"

"Thanks Bernie. I'd rather wait until tomorrow."

"No problem. I'll set it up."

"Thank you. I'd appreciate that," Tate said, shaking hands with her and Sergeant Adams as they left his small apartment.

He stared at Vicki. He remembered her. He did. But he was surprised that he wasn't feeling a surge of joy or affection or lust. They were married. He should be feeling something. He guiltily thought of Alyson. Ten minutes away from her and he was overcome with all sorts of emotions and desires and wants when she walked back into the room. If he had married Vicki, he obviously must have felt that same passion for her at some point. Some things were still a little fuzzy in his memory. Perhaps he simply needed more time. All of this was quite a bit to absorb.

As though reading his mind she said, "Do you remember what we were talking about on the phone the day you disappeared?"

He closed his eyes and pushed the image of the plane crashing into the building out of his head. He tried to focus his thoughts back to before that moment. He could remember they had been arguing.

"You were upset," he said. "You were yelling and crying and hysterical."

"Do you remember why?"

Tate tried to remember. "We lost the baby."

"Yes. We did. But that was a year before."

"Yes. Right. I can't remember why you were upset. I remember losing the baby. We didn't try again?"

"No. We didn't."

"So I don't have a child?"

"No, Tate. I'm sorry."

"I'm kind of relieved. I would have missed so much. I would have put that child, just like I put you and my family and friends through the hell of thinking I was dead. I just couldn't remember. Everything went blank. All I knew was that I was scared and I was running. I thought I was running from someone but I suppose I was running from the horror of the unimaginable things I had witnessed that day."

"You suffered severe psychological trauma, Tate. I'm sure your doctors will help you figure out what happened."

"So what were we talking about?"

Vicki gave him a sad smile, "I'm afraid I added to your distress that day. I had filed for divorce and that morning I found the papers that you had signed on the kitchen table. I guess I was upset that you didn't want to fight for me. I know that's crazy. I was the one who had insisted on a divorce. But seeing your signature on the papers that morning made me a little crazy. I felt the need to lash out at you. I was screaming at you Tate. Saying hateful, hurtful things to you. And then you just disappeared. I am so sorry."

Tate didn't say anything. Just sat and stared at the floor.

"Please say something," she pleaded.

"It's okay, Vick. I'm kind of relieved. I didn't feel the level of joy I would expect to feel when I realized who you were. I guess that explains it."

"Yeah. After I lost the baby we drifted apart."

"It was difficult. You were almost to term."

"Yeah. And the baby was really the only reason we got married. We tried to do the right things but we ended up making each other miserable. And when we lost the baby it completely destroyed us. We drifted further and further apart every day."

"I'm sorry I didn't try harder, Vick."

"It takes two, Tate. I didn't try either."

"Have you moved on?"

"Yes. You had already signed the papers so I filed them eventually. I honestly thought you had been in that building. Your appointment was on the floor above where the plane struck. You would not have survived that."

"Oh my God. I was running late that morning. I missed the early train and then stopped to take your call. I almost ignored it you know. You probably saved my life."

"When I saw your photo plastered all over the news, I couldn't believe it. I still can't believe that you're alive and well. Dave is going to be so excited. I wouldn't be surprised if he's on his way here too."

"Oh God. How is he?" Tate asked, hit broadside by a flood of memories about his best friend since middle school.

"We haven't stayed in touch. I think he's in Seattle but I haven't seen him since your memorial."

"You had a memorial for me?"

"Of course I did."

"That must have been so hard on Mom and Dad."

"They didn't come. They refused to accept your death. They didn't make me feel guilty for moving on but they never gave up on the hope that you had survived. They even hired a private investigator to look for you but there simply weren't any leads."

"Really? God that must have been so hard on them."

"It was," she said, reaching out to squeeze his arm.

Tate cleared his throat, "So you're married now? Happy? Do you have kids?"

"I am. He's a great guy. I think you guys would really like each other. I have two boys. They're twelve and eight. Little terrors but I love them to pieces."

"I bet you do. I'm happy for you, Vick."

"Thanks, Tate. How about you? Is there anyone in your life now?"

He thought of Alyson. God he hoped she was still in his life. "There hadn't been. No."

"What about the woman who was here when we arrived?"

"She is a long story. Perhaps one best saved for another day."

"Of course. I'll head back to the hotel."

"I'm sorry I don't have a car or I'd drive you. I can call you a cab though and cover your fare."

"No worries. I have my phone. Tate, one more thing."

"Yes?"

"Even though I had to accept that you were most likely dead, part of me never stopped hoping that your parents were right. Since becoming a parent myself I think I understand a little better now why they felt so strongly that you didn't die. I feel that same connection to my kids, almost a sixth sense when they're sick or in trouble. They refused to have you counted among the dead that day."

Tate wiped tears from his eyes. "Thanks for telling me that, Vick. You're still an amazing woman. You always were."

"Thanks," she whispered, brushing tears off her cheeks. "Are you going to be okay?"

"I am," he said. "How about you?"

"Yeah. I'll be fine. I'm going to stay for a couple of days in case you need anything but then I'll head back home." She jotted down her cell number and the contact details for his father's nursing home.

"Thank you for coming to see me. You didn't have to do that."

"Yeah, Tate. I really did."

She squeezed his hand and let herself out. Tate stared at the door for a moment and then grabbed the piece of paper Vicki had left him. Taking a deep breath he dialed the nursing home number and spoke with the director of the centre, explaining who he was and apologizing for having been out of touch. He was connected to the nursing station closest to his dad and the nurse who answered advised him his father was resting comfortably. It had been a good day. He had gone for a walk around the lake and fed the ducks. Tate promised that he would visit as soon as he could.

He hung up and felt a fresh wave of tears start. He had missed so much. His parents had never given up hope that he was alive. He was aching to visit his mother's grave and talk to her. Tell her how much he loved her. How thankful he was for having her in his life. He wanted to tell her that she had been an incredible mother and his best friend.

He started making a list for Bernie. In order for him to travel to New York he would need a passport. That should be easier now that he knew his identity. Of course the fifteen year absence might complicate the hell out of everything. Bernie would help him cut through some of the bureaucracy. He needed to book a plane ticket.

Dave. He wanted to hear Dave's voice. He called information and asked for Dave Harrison's number in Seattle. There were four hits. Dammit. He asked for all four numbers and started dialing. The first two weren't the right Dave. On the third call a young child picked up.

"Hello. May I speak with your daddy please?" Tate asked, his voice shaking.

"Daaaaaaaddddyyyy!" the young voice screamed directly into the phone.

He could hear a man chuckling as the little voice said, "Here you go Daddy."

"Hello," Dave said.

Tate closed his eyes. It was Dave. He was in Seattle. Vicki got it right.

"Dave. It's me. It's Tate."

He was greeted by a long moment of silence.

"Dave, man, you still there? I know this is a shock but it's me. I'm back. I'm okay." Tate cleared his throat as he struggled to contain his joy at reconnecting with his best friend after fifteen years.

"Oh God. I'm dreaming. I'm dreaming and I can't wake up."

"It's not a dream, bro. It's really me."

"Tate? What? Oh my God. Tate! Is it really you?" Dave asked, his voice breaking.

"Yes. It's really me."

"What the hell man? How is this possible? Jesus! Where have you been?"

"I've been lost. No memory. It's a long story. You didn't see my story in the news?"

"I've been overseas on business. Just got home about an hour ago. Why were you in the news?"

"The local police thought a media blitz would be my best shot at having someone recognize me. It worked. Vicki saw my photo and came here to confirm it was really me."

"Holy shit. I can't believe this. We thought you'd died that day, bro. It was the worst day of my life."

"I'm sorry about that. I can now remember seeing the first plane hit the tower and then people starting jumping Dave. It was too much. I guess I had some kind of breakdown. My mind just shut down. I just started walking. My memory is really patchy for the first few years. I can remember waking up on a park bench in upstate New York with no idea of who I was or where I was from. I don't even know how I got that far. I always felt afraid and like I was running from something. That's how I've been living for the last decade and a half."

"Christ. That's incredible. All this time and you've been alive."

"I know. It's crazy."

"Why didn't you try the media blitz before?"

"I never reported to the authorities before. I was too scared. I was terrified that I had done something wrong and was running from something, like the police."

"Oh my God. Where have you been living all this time?"

"I was homeless. Roaming from town to town. Squatting wherever I could and taking whatever menial jobs I could get without identification. Right now I'm in Newfoundland, Canada."

"God, Tate", Dave took a deep breath, "Sounds like you've had a rough go of it bro."

"There were definitely rough patches. It's a long story and I'll fill you in when we're face to face. I just needed to hear your voice. You know about Mom?"

"Yeah, bud. I went to her funeral. It was like losing my own mom."

"She loved you like a son."

"She was an amazing lady. I loved her dearly."

"You know about Dad?"

"Yeah. I visit him twice a year but he doesn't know me now. I'm so sorry, Tate."

"I'm going to see him as soon as I can get a passport in place. Not sure how much red tape I'll face given the circumstances."

"I'll make some calls and see if I can help from this end. Let me know when you plan to visit your dad. I'll fly out and see you."

"Thanks, Dave. You've always had my back."

"You've always had mine. Tate?"

"Yeah Dave?"

"I love you, bro."

"I love you, too. See you real soon."

Tate hung up and was hit broadside by a fresh wave of emotion. He wasn't completely alone in the world after all. He had Dave. He had his dad. He hoped he still had Alyson. He should call her. Part of him really wanted to but another part needed a few hours to himself. He was still reeling from all that had happened and he was exhausted. He needed time to process all of these memories. All of this new information. He would touch base with her tomorrow after his appointment with Dr. Tucker. He'd have a better idea of what he was dealing with then. He was hopeful that he wouldn't suffer from memory loss again but he had no idea how his brain was wired or what to expect. Dr. Tucker would hopefully have some answers.

He brushed his teeth, pulled off his clothes and fell into bed feeling exhausted but exhilarated. It was incredible. He wasn't John Smith. He wasn't lost anymore. He was Tate Sampson. Architect. Son. Friend. He was someone.

CHAPTER 25

Alyson groaned as she rolled over in her bed, her head throbbing, her body shaking. Shit. The mother of all hangovers. Her mouth was dry, her tongue felt swollen and her head was going to burst any moment. She tried to sit up and her stomach lurched. She knew she wouldn't make it to the bathroom so she vomited on the floor next to her bed. She was grateful the floors were hardwood and not carpeted. The putrid smell of the regurgitated wine was so vile that she threw up again, repeatedly until there was nothing but acidic bile burning the back of her throat.

She gingerly rolled to the other side of the bed and hauled herself upright, taking slow, shaky steps to the bathroom. She rinsed her mouth and swallowed two Tylenol. Grabbing a large towel she went back to the room and threw it over the vomit. It smelled horrible. She'd have to clean it up sooner, not later. Retribution was a bitch.

She made her way downstairs, turned on the kettle and went to the laundry room to fill a bucket with soapy water. She noticed something blue on the counter. It was a tee-shirt. A man's tee-shirt. John's shirt. No. That wasn't right. His name was Tate. Not John. Would she ever get used to that? She lifted the shirt to her face but it smelled like her laundry detergent. There was no trace of John/Tate remaining. She wiped tears from her eyes, shocked that she had any left to shed after the deluge overnight.

She wondered if he was in bed with his wife. She wanted to feel happy for him but she was shattered by her own sense of loss. It was overwhelming. It overshadowed everything else at the moment. His wife was beautiful. Tall, willowy with red curly hair and dark brown eyes. She was surprised he had forgotten her. And she had seemed so shocked at seeing him alive and well. Alyson couldn't even imagine what the poor woman had been through. And the jolt of recognizing his face on the news must have been a heart wrenching moment.

She selfishly wished they had waited until after the holidays to go to the police. She should have stolen just a little more time with him. She knew that didn't say much about her but for the first time in a long time she had felt joy again. She had felt cherished and desired and hope had blossomed inside of her.

Alyson sighed and faced the mess she had made on her bedroom floor. She swore to herself as she cleaned up the vomit that she would never drink again. Yeah, right. Like that would happen. Okay, maybe she wouldn't drink that much again. Yeah. That was a promise she was more likely to keep.

She sipped on tea and waited for the Tylenol to kick in. When she felt a little more balanced she took a shower and felt marginally better. She walked through the house, realizing for the first time how big and empty it really was for one person. Tate's absence echoed through every room. There was still an indentation in the pillow on the sofa he favoured. She had no plans to ever move it or fluff it again. His scent lingered on the sheets in the guest room and she knew she'd have to change them eventually but not yet. She had filled her house with beautiful furniture and tasteful art but it wasn't filled with laughter and love and the chaos of a family. That's what the house really needed. That's what she really needed.

"It's time, Joe," she whispered. "It's time to find love again and start that family we had dreamed of when we were together." She felt that pull of sadness that she always felt when she realized the enormity of what she had lost when that drunk driver had hit and killed her husband.

She thought of John. *Dammit.* Tate. His life had been taken away too. He had lost fifteen years with his wife and loved ones. At least he had a second chance now. She wondered if she'd see him before he returned to his newly remembered life. She had kind of expected him to call by now but she figured that might be a little difficult, and inappropriate, while snuggling with his wife. She couldn't let her mind go there. It hurt too much. It was no more than she deserved for sleeping with him when she didn't know whether he was married. Even so, the pain of losing him was suffocating.

She had to get out of the house. Her foot wasn't strong enough to go hiking but she could drive into the city and finish her Christmas shopping. She had to buy replacement gloves for her dad since she had given the ones she had already bought to Tate. *Tate.* She liked the name. It suited him. Strong. Succinct. Not common.

God! Every thought went back to him. She had to distract herself. She pulled on a sweater and twisted her hair into a loose braid and left the house. The temperature had been warming up and the snow was melting. Newfoundland weather was consistently unpredictable. She had been thoroughly charmed when she first moved here by how the locals loved to talk about the weather. In their defense, it usually was talk-worthy.

She made a mental list of items she needed to purchase as she drove to the city. As much as she loved downtown shopping she decided to hit the mall instead; less likely chance of bumping into Tate. And his wife. There was a perfume she wanted to buy for her mom and she had to decide on a gift for

Syd, maybe a bracelet. She always gave Lois goofy pajamas and a current bestselling novel. Her list was very short. She was looking forward to the day when she'd have nieces and nephews to spoil, and children of her own.

She found the perfect gifts right away but didn't want to return to her big, empty house. She browsed the Christmas themed stores, buying garlands and ornaments for a tree she was determined to decorate this year. She bought gift-wrap and ribbons and mistletoe. It seemed extravagant to do all of that for just herself but she was tired of being sad and defeated. Now that she'd had a taste of happiness again, it had whetted her appetite for more. She wasn't kidding herself; she knew the sadness still lurked and would kick her ass plenty in the days, weeks and months to come. But she was hopeful that the joyful days would outnumber the bad ones. Time for that tide to turn in her favour.

She toted her packages to her car and stowed them in the trunk. She treated herself to a burger at a nearby fast food drive-through and ate in the car, listening to a local radio station while she watched people coming and going in the busy parking lot. Young parents with kids in tow looked weary and exhausted. She envied them. Her biological clock was throttling into overdrive today.

She still wasn't ready to go home. She needed a job or a volunteer position. She needed something to focus her time and energy on besides her personal life and loss. Well, make that losses now that Tate was added to the tally. *Tate.* In a flash of inspiration, she pulled out her phone and did a quick Google search. There was a shelter for the homeless in the downtown core. Maybe she'd pop in and see if she could volunteer her time or make a donation. She pulled out of the mall area and headed south to the harbour district, excited to have thought of volunteering. She realized that really that's what had been missing in her life since moving here; a sense of purpose. A reason to get out of bed in the morning. She liked the idea of making a positive difference in some way.

She arrived at the shelter just as the volunteers were cleaning up the pots and pans from the meals they had prepared for that day. There were close to fifty people inside. She wondered if that was typical. One of the volunteers pointed out the manager of the shelter, a woman named Sue, who looked to be in her mid-forties. She was speaking with a patron and exuded a warm and boisterous personality. Alyson liked her instantly. She waited until Sue had finished her conversation and then approached her.

"Hi Sue. My name is Alyson Fisher and I'm interested in volunteering at your shelter."

"Hi Alyson. That's great. Let's go to my office and chat."

"Thank you."

"Tell me why you'd like to volunteer here," Sue asked, after they were seated in her small office at the back of the building.

"A man without a home recently saved my life and I really want to give back. I want to make a difference, somehow."

"That's a great reason. Let me grab you an application form. You also have to provide a Certificate of Conduct and a Vulnerable Sector Check. You can apply for those from the local police."

"I actually have those already. I needed them for something else." Alyson didn't elaborate that a couple of months ago she had started looking into the adoption process. She and Joe had planned to have their own children but they also dreamed of adopting a child. The papers were still in the bottom drawer of her filing cabinet. It was a big decision and she wasn't sure if she was strong enough to be a parent without Joe.

"Great! That simplifies everything. Can you email them over to me this afternoon?"

"Absolutely. Is it okay if I fill out your form now?"

"Of course. Here's a pen. Just use the edge of my desk."

The form was basic and Alyson completed it in a few minutes and passed it back to Sue.

Sue quickly reviewed it. "When can you start, Alyson?"

"Immediately. Tomorrow. Whenever you need me."

"Fantastic. How about ten tomorrow? You can do a trial shift and if you like it we can give you a schedule."

"That's perfect."

"Come on. Let me show you around."

They moved through the common room and into the kitchen. Alyson was really impressed with the scale of the operation. They offered classes in literacy and life skills and provided space for a nurse practitioner and social worker to visit twice weekly.

"How long have you managed the shelter, Sue?"

Sue smiled, "Five years this month. But before that I was really down on my luck and used to come here for a meal and to warm up now and then. The happiest day of my life was the day I had turned my life around to the point where I could accept this job."

"Good for you. That's a fabulous story. Do you have many regulars?"

"We do, mostly elderly folks. Many of them don't even have proper winter coats or boots. We do what we can but we rely heavily on donations."

"What do you need?"

"Everything really. Coats, boots, warm gloves and hats. All of the usual winter gear."

"Thank you so much for the opportunity. I'm excited to start tomorrow."

"We are so happy to have you. We could use a few extra volunteers and you indicated on your form that you were available daily. That's exactly what we need."

They said goodbye and Alyson returned to her car excited that she could finally focus on something that wasn't completely about her and what she had lost. The rest of the day loomed ahead of her and she was reluctant to return to her empty house. She smiled as she realized there was something else she could do right now.

She returned to the chaos of the mall and her step was light as she pushed a cart through a general merchandise store. When she filled that cart she took it to the checkouts and asked if they would hold the items until she finished shopping. She filled four carts in total. She bought jackets and boots in several sizes, as well as the other items Sue had mentioned. She spent thousands of dollars and it felt good. Joe had left her more money than she could possibly need in two lifetimes. She felt grateful to have the means to help others. It took her four trips to bring all of the clothing items to her car. She drove straight back to the shelter and started hauling the bags inside. Sue was dumbfounded and hugged her and thanked her repeatedly.

"No thanks necessary," she said. "As I mentioned earlier, a man without a home recently saved my life. It's my pleasure to give back."

"You are an angel, Alyson Fisher," Sue said, smiling through her tears.

"No, Sue. I was a lost soul who suddenly has purpose. Thank you for that."

She drove home, exhausted and more content than she had felt in a very long time.

CHAPTER 26

Tate hadn't slept more than an hour for the entire night. Now that the memories were flooding back they were consuming him and he was swept away in the cataclysm. He remembered the first time he had gone fishing with his dad. He was probably five years old and he landed a huge trout. He could still hear his dad's roar of delight echoing out across the lake. He remembered how much his mom had loved Christmas. He had been an only child and she had been worried he was lonely. When he was six she talked his dad into letting her get him a puppy. It was a chocolate lab and Tate named him Chip, because chocolate chips were his favourite candy. He remembered his mom laughing at his reasoning and declaring it was a fine name. He'd had that dog until his early 20s. Losing Chip had been like losing a member of the family.

He remembered the first day he had met Dave. They had both started a new school their first year of junior high. Their lockers were next to each other and they had several classes together. Their friendship had been natural and they became inseparable. They saw each other through the awkward puberty years, crushes, lost ball games, championship victories, fights, and first loves. Dave had four younger sisters so he often sought refuge at the Sampson household, and they were happy to welcome him. He became like a brother to Tate. They had been each other's best men at their respective weddings. He could remember breaking down when he toasted Dave at his wedding to Zara, his beautiful African goddess. He had intended to do a roast but he took one look at his best friend and his joy and love on his wedding day were undeniable. Tate finished his toast with a sappy, emotional thank you for being the brother he never had and the best friend any one could ever hope to find. Dave stood and hugged him and his eyes had been wet too.

He remembered his first real girlfriend and how awkward he felt kissing her for the first time. She had been a summer crush, a classmate's older cousin visiting from out of state for the entire month of July. He had thought his heart would beat out of his chest the first time he had slipped his hand under her tee shirt. She had been a couple years older and slightly more experienced than him. She encouraged him to move much faster than he would have felt comfortable doing on his own. But hey, he was sixteen and she was offering him everything he had been fantasizing about for the past two years. Of course he was going to unwrap that gift and enjoy it to the fullest. And he did. He was clumsy and unskilled and lasted literally seconds the night he gave her his virginity in the back of her aunt's car. His lover had been patient and kind though. She assured him that was normal and to wait a few minutes and try again. The second time was marginally better. By the end of summer she had taught him everything she knew, which in retrospect hadn't been all that much. They figured out a few other things together. Thanks to her, he no longer felt awkward or unskilled through the balance of his high school years. He couldn't remember her name but he could still picture her lovely face and long black hair. Dark and shiny like Alyson's hair.

Tate's phone rang, shaking him from his reverie. He reached for it, willing the caller to be Alyson. It was Bernie. He swallowed back his disappointment as she confirmed his appointment with Dr. Tucker for noon and said she was working with the American Consulate to get a passport for him so he could return to New York. Tate thanked her and hung up.

He felt a surge of sadness at the thought of leaving this place and especially leaving Alyson. He wondered if she would consider visiting him. He would definitely visit her, if she'd have him. He missed her. He wondered if she was missing him, too. He hoped so. He fought the impulse to call her. He wanted to meet with his doctor first.

He opened his drapes and was happy to see sunshine streaming in through his window. The street below looked busy as office workers and Christmas shoppers rushed by. Everyone had somewhere they had to be it seemed. He smiled to himself. So did he. He was Tate Sampson and he had to get ready to visit his doctor. He headed to the shower feeling like the weight of the world had been lifted from his shoulders. He wasn't a felon. He hadn't committed a heinous crime. He wasn't running from the law.

The truth was equally horrible though. He had witnessed an atrocious act of terror. He forced the images from his thoughts. He had lost so much of his life that day. With the loss of his memory came the precious lost years with his aging parents. He was so deeply sorry for that. But he was still here. Thousands had perished that day. Senselessly. He was somehow still alive with a second chance to live a better life. He felt a deep sense of responsibility to do just that. Live a life that made a positive difference in the world in honour of all of those who weren't able to simply walk away that day. He owed them that. He owed the universe that for sparing him.

Bernie had insisted on giving Tate a ride to his appointment. She was anxious to hear how he was feeling and whether his memories had completely returned. Tate filled her in on the high level details, still amazed himself by how instantaneously he returned to himself. She dropped him off saying she had another appointment in the area and she'd be back in an hour to pick him up.

Dr. Tucker greeted Tate with a warm handshake and a genuine smile.

"Good afternoon, Tate. Bernie tells me you've had quite an evening," Dr. Tucker said.

"Good afternoon, Dr. Tucker. Yeah, that's a bit of an understatement."

"Come in and grab a seat. Would you like something to drink?" he asked.

"Just water, please," Tate replied, sinking into one of the two wing chairs opposite the desk.

Dr. Tucker pulled two bottles of water from a small fridge in his office and handing one to Tate, uncapped his own bottle and took a sip as he lowered himself into the second armchair.

"So the media appeal worked. Your wife recognized you in the paper and flew here yesterday?"

"Yes. Except she's my ex-wife but seeing her made all of the memories come rushing back. It was incredible."

"I bet it was. That's amazing. How are you feeling about everything now? Are there memory gaps? Periods you can't remember?"

"I can remember pretty much everything except the days immediately following the attack. I can remember seeing the plane hit and people jumping from the building. I think I can remember walking but I can't remember where I was going. I just wanted to get away from there. My next memory is waking on a park bench in upstate New York with no wallet or identification. I'm not sure how I got there or even what day it was and I couldn't remember that bit until last night. But I think I can remember most things after that."

"That's excellent. It might be a good idea to jot down what you can remember from that time just for your own interest. Document where you've been and the jobs you took on and any memorable people you met. It's very unusual to have such a long period of amnesia, not impossible but definitely not common."

"I'll do that. Do you think my memories will vanish again?"

"I suspect you most likely suffered from dissociative fugue. That is basically a reversible amnesia that was triggered by the psychological trauma of witnessing the terrorist attack. It is typically temporary and short lived but it can, as in your case, last for years. It's rare but possible."

"Will I require treatment or therapy going forward?"

"No. Your memories should continue to fill in. You might never regain those hours immediately following the incident but even they might return at some point. If you feel stress or anxiety dealing with the loss of the last fifteen years or the trauma that caused the amnesia, then by all means, seek therapy. But otherwise, your mind should naturally take care of itself now that the process has started."

"It is astounding that my brain could actually do that. Simply shut off to avoid dealing with the horror of what I had experienced that day."

"Your mind was protecting you. Your compulsion to move around is another indicator of dissociative fugue, as is forgetting your identity."

"So that's it. I simply snapped out of it?"

"Pretty much, yes. From what Bernie relayed last night, seeing your ex-wife was the catalyst to bring you out of the fugue state. If you experience memory lapses I want you to contact me but Tate, it would be unusual to have a relapse. I'm pretty confident you're in the clear."

"That's awesome news, Dr. Tucker. Thank you so much."

"All the best to you, Tate." They shook hands and Tate left his office, feeling once again like an incredible burden had been lifted. He actually felt lighter. Bernie hadn't returned so he stepped outside to wait for her, enjoying the feel of the sunshine on his skin. She pulled up a few minutes later and flashed him her big, bright smile when he climbed into her car.

"I have good news," she beamed.

"Oh?" Tate said, a little surprised that the good news kept rolling in when for so many years there had been no news and bad luck. All of that changed with Alyson. His life changed the moment he met her. That was undeniable.

"The American Consulate heard from a friend of yours, Dave Harrison. He's willing to serve as an Identifying Witness for you. That basically means he'll give a sworn affidavit regarding your identity and the circumstances that lead to your amnesia. Your ex-wife contacted me a few moments ago and offered to do the same. This will expedite the process. There will still be some hiccups but we'll work through those."

"That's awesome news, Bernie. I've come to think of you as my miracle worker."

"Ha! Not at all. You did the hard work. You put your image out there and faced the uncertainty of what would happen."

"I'm relieved I haven't been recognized locally since that incident at the restaurant."

"The hat and dark glasses you're wearing may have something to do with that," Bernie teased.

"True but I thought that only worked in the movies," he chuckled.

"Do you need to run any other errands or shall I drive you back to your place?" she asked.

"My place is fine. Thanks for everything, Bernie."

"It has been my pleasure. And I will get you back home to see your dad too. I promise you that."

"I've never doubted you for a moment," he smiled at her, touched by the extent of her kindness. Sure it was her job but he had a feeling she went above and beyond for all of her clients. He felt very blessed to have been assigned to her.

As soon as he got back to his place he called Alyson's home number. She didn't answer. He tried her cell but she didn't pick up there either. He had a sinking feeling that she was avoiding him. He paced his small apartment for a while but felt confined in the tiny space. He donned his simple disguise again and headed outside for a walk. The crisp air would help clear his mind. He headed down a couple of streets to Duckworth and Water, to browse the eclectic gift shops housed in century old buildings, some faced with bright, colourful clapboard and others with brick. Most of the storefronts were decorated for the holidays and the snow lined sidewalks lent an air of postcard worthiness to the scene. It felt rather like Dickensville as he merged seamlessly with the other shoppers. It was odd not feeling like the sore thumb in a crowd. He had rarely felt as though he belonged anywhere. That had changed with Alyson too. He owed her so much. He hoped she would answer his calls later. He had so much news to share with her. He couldn't believe that she would deliberately ignore him. She was too kind and gracious to do that. She was probably just busy.

He went into a small store that featured handmade wooden items. A series of frames caught his attention. They were intricately carved yet not ornate. They were perfect. He deliberated over them for several long moments, finally choosing one to purchase. He had an idea for a gift for Alyson. He would have to work quickly as he didn't know how much time he had before returning to New York. He felt excitement at the prospect of creating something for her and realized he needed a few other items for his project. He explained to the clerk what he was looking for and she was very helpful in providing directions to a nearby shop.

He headed out the door with a spring in his step. He chuckled aloud when he realized he had become one of those people rushing along the streets in search of the perfect gift that he had observed from his window earlier. He rather enjoyed this return to normalcy.

CHAPTER 27

Alyson arrived at the shelter almost an hour before her shift was scheduled to start. There were only a handful of people in the common room and the kitchen was locked so she couldn't start the meal preparations. Truthfully, she wouldn't know where to start anyway. It would take a while to learn the ropes. There were a few patrons sitting in the lounge area seeking shelter from the crisp air outside. She said hello to each of them and paused a moment to ask them how they were. Some of them eyed her warily, suspicious of her interest in them. Others were engaging and eager to chat. One woman was deliberately abrasive.

"What the hell are you doin' slummin' here, Princess?" she asked, her deeply lined face twisting into a sneer. She was perhaps five feet tall and looked to be underweight, yet she drew herself to her full height and despite being shorter than Alyson, still somehow managed to look down her nose at her.

"Now Nellie," one of the men sitting next to the door came to Alyson's defense, "don't scare the pretty young thing away. She's just here to help."

"Hmph," the ornery woman named Nellie grunted. "Scare her away. She won't last an hour here, not that one."

Alyson smiled at Nellie and said, "We'll see about that, Miss Nellie."

Nellie grunted again and walked to the far side of the room to talk to a couple of women who were watching the scene unfold and chuckling to themselves.

Alyson wondered what Nellie's situation was and how she and the others here had ended up homeless. She thought of Tate and wondered how many facilities like this he had used over the years. She wondered if any of these people had families waiting for them, not knowing they were alive. Circumstances were rarely as simple as they seemed and she imagined that many of these people had stories that would rip her heart out. She noticed that a couple of the men were wearing some of the items she had purchased yesterday. And skeptical Nellie was sporting the bright green scarf and glove set Alyson had added, hoping the whimsy might appeal to someone. She was delighted that she could help in some small way and it made her want to do more.

Lucy, the kitchen supervisor, arrived and her day suddenly shifted into overdrive. Her foot was a little achy and she realized she was probably overdoing it but she didn't care. She wanted to ensure these wonderful folks had a hot, nutritious meal. She chopped vegetables for soup until her arms ached. And then she chopped some more. She mixed a glaze for the six hams arranged in three huge roasting pans and peeled potatoes for a casserole, cutting them into thin slices as directed by Lucy. They had a dozen volunteers in the kitchen and every one of them was as busy or busier than Alyson. It was a bustling spot. They were expecting close to one hundred people for meals throughout the day so they wanted to ensure they had enough.

The volunteers, ten women including Alyson, a middle aged man with a hearty laugh, and a young man named Jake chatted amicably while they worked. Alyson really liked the vibe in the centre. It radiated goodness, care and concern. Surprisingly that spirit lasted the entire shift, through the serving and interacting with the patrons, even grumpy Nellie, and through the messy cleanup to follow. Everyone was tired but smiling. It was addictive and she knew she would be back. She wanted to be added to the regular schedule. Lucy was delighted with her commitment for additional shifts and they worked out a two-week schedule.

When she got to her car she checked her phone. No missed calls. She was a little disappointed. She had missed a couple of calls from Tate yesterday but when she tried calling him back he hadn't picked up. She hoped he was okay. Maybe she should try his number again. She tried to ignore the butterflies that had taken up residence in her stomach at the thought of hearing his voice. She had no reason to be nervous anymore. He was married and would be leaving. End of story. Still, if there was something he needed, she wanted to be there for him. She tried his number but there was no answer. She'd try again later after she arrived home.

She had one more stop to make before heading to her place. She wanted to buy something for Tate for Christmas. She had been thinking about what to get him all day but nothing had come to mind. Just before she left the shelter she had a moment of inspiration. She would buy him a journal to record his memories going forward, and record those he just recently remembered. That way if he had any further memory issues, the journal might help him recover faster. At least she hoped that's the way his mind worked.

She thought of his beautiful sketches and decided to drive to a local art supply store and browse the well-stocked shop. She found an old fashioned fountain pen. It wasn't very practical for journal writing but there was something charming about it. She decided to get it for him along with a high quality bottled ink recommended by the clerk. She moved to the section on journals. They had several types to choose from ranging from cardboard covers to intricately embossed leather bound books.

The one that stood out to her had a cognac coloured leather cover etched with a border of Celtic knots. The pages were heavy and lined on one side, blank on the other. Perfect for recording memories and sketching. She noticed that anytime he sketched he used black pencils so she picked up a package of water colour pencils as well and a more practical pen. She paid for her purchases and left the store holding a small paper sack laden with treasure. She hoped he would like the items.

As soon as she got home she poured herself a glass of wine. She went upstairs to the study where she had stashed the wrapping paper, ribbons and gift boxes she'd recently purchased. She lugged the large bag of supplies back to the kitchen, taking extra care on the stairs with her footing. The last thing she needed was another injury. She set everything up on the kitchen island, settling on a stool as she removed the gifts she had selected for Tate from the paper bag. She wrapped each item in brightly coloured tissue paper before placing them in a plain white gift box. She then selected a decorative red and green plaid ribbon and tied it around the box. It was simple but festive. She looked forward to giving him the gift.

She fished her cell phone out of her purse and tried his number again but there still wasn't any answer. She belatedly wondered if perhaps he had tried her house line and was happy to see that the message indicator light was blinking. She played back the message but it wasn't Tate, it was actually Bernie asking her to return her call. With shaking hands, Alyson dialed the number, praying nothing bad had happened to Tate.

Bernie answered on the second ring, obviously recognizing Alyson's number because she greeted her by name.

"Is everything okay with Tate?" Alyson asked.

"Yes, better than okay actually," Bernie said. "Given the extraordinary circumstances of his situation, the American

Embassy was able to arrange temporary identification for Tate to allow him to fly to their Consulate office in Halifax. You probably know there is no U.S. embassy office in Newfoundland."

"Actually, no, I had no idea."

"In any case, they expect to issue a temporary passport in the next couple of days to allow him to return to New York. He flew to Halifax last night."

"What? He's gone? Already? " Alyson leaned against the wall for support. He was gone. She could feel herself deflating.

"He really wanted to see you and tried to reach you but there wasn't any answer at either of your phones."

"I was out all day yesterday and went to bed early," Alyson explained. "So he's really gone?"

"Yes. Vicki flew out with him last night. He wanted me to thank you for everything and said he would be in touch as soon as possible."

"Thank you for letting me know."

"My pleasure. Take care, Alyson. And Merry Christmas."

"Merry Christmas to you, Bernie," Alyson said, hanging up the phone just before the torrent of tears started. He was gone. Not even a goodbye. Of course he had tried but the universe had other plans. Maybe it was better this way. Maybe it would be less painful not to have seen him again. Maybe such an abrupt departure would help her in her quest to move on.

If all that were true, why did she feel like someone had just ripped out her heart and stomped all over it? She threw his gift in the bag with the supplies and lugged it back upstairs. She crawled into the bed in the guest room and pulled the sheets around her, inhaling the faint trace of his scent. It was fading and it was all that she had left of him.

CHAPTER 28

Tate hugged Vicki goodbye at LaGuardia, thanking her for all that she had done for him. She had even accompanied him to Halifax to help him get his temporary passport. She had really gone above and beyond and he appreciated her help and support. He rushed outside the terminal and hailed a cab. He was anxious to see his dad. He gave the address to the cab driver and sat back, clutching his battered pack. It still held everything that he owned in the world, though he supposed that would change now.

The cab ride felt like it was taking forever. He had already become used to the relatively short distances when travelling from one side of the city to the other in St. John's. New York was gargantuan in comparison and traffic was not comparable by any stretch of the imagination. After a fifty-five minute drive they finally arrived at the long term care facility. Tate paid the fare and eagerly approached the front door. The receptionist inside was surprised to hear that he was Mr. Sampson's son. She said that there was no record of family. Tate showed the woman his temporary passport.

"If you look in my dad's file there should be an email from the American Consulate verifying my identity."

The receptionist called up his father's electronic file and her eyes widened in surprise as she read the note.

"I'm sorry Mr. Sampson. I just came on shift and no one had mentioned this email. I'll have someone show you to your father's room. Please sign in here."

"Thank you," Tate said, scrawling his name in the registry book along with the date and time. He looked at his signature and shook his head in amazement. Until two days ago he hadn't signed his name in fifteen years, yet his scrawled signature came readily. It felt as natural as though he had been signing it every day since then. How odd.

A young man approached Tate and offered to show him to his dad's room. Tate felt anxious and his heart was pounding. He knew Dave had wanted to be here, and he had let him know he was flying in this evening, but on such short notice the best Dave could do was a flight leaving Seattle at midnight. Tate had told him to wait until the next day but he wouldn't hear of it. Dave booked two rooms in a hotel near the nursing home and told him he'd meet him there early the next day. At least Tate had a place to go for the night after the visit.

His dad had a private room. The facility was nice. It was borderline posh actually. It appeared comfortable, clean and well staffed. His initial impressions were all positive. His father was sleeping and Tate nearly doubled over in pain when he saw how old and frail he looked. He was only seventy years old but he looked at least a decade older. Perhaps two. He had lost weight and his stature seemed much slighter than Tate remembered. His once black hair was completely silver and his face was sunken. Tate wondered how many lonely hours he must have spent since losing his mother. With both her and Tate gone he had no family nearby. He felt a surge of gratitude to Dave and Vicki for continuing to visit him over the years.

"Dad. It's me, Tate," he gently shook his father's arm, and ran his hand over his still thick hair.

His father stirred, his eyes fluttering open.

"Oh hello," he said. "You came."

"Yes, Dad. I came to see you. Sorry it took so long."

"Who are you? I think I know you. Do I know you?"

"Yes, Dad. I'm your son. Tate. I was away for a long time but I'm back now. I'm back to stay." Tate's voice was thick with the heartbreak of the lost years that had changed everything.

His father looked at him blankly and then he said, "Tate. My son. Oh that's nice. Is it sunny outside?"

Tate realized with a heavy heart that his dad didn't recognize him. He didn't know him. Of course he wouldn't but some small part of him had secretly hoped that his sudden reappearance might spark some flash of memory or recognition. "No, Dad. It's not sunny. It's night time now so it's dark outside."

"That's nice," his dad said. "Do I know you?"

Tate smiled at his father and blinked back his tears, "I think you know me, Dad. I'm Tate. I'm your son."

His father sized him up for several long minutes and said, "Tate. Tate. You remind me of someone. Do I know you?"

He took his father's hand in his and sat on the chair next to the bed, repeating the answer to the question his dad would ask dozens of times in their two hour visit. Tate knew he didn't understand the words and would forget them as soon as they were spoken but at the very least he hoped his father would feel his love.

The nursing staff asked him if he'd mind coming back in the morning as it was important that his dad get his proper rest. They told him that routine was really important to his mental state and he was calmer and more content when his schedule was maintained. Tate was reluctant to leave but didn't want to do anything to cause his father any more discomfort or grief than he had already inflicted. His absence was inadvertent but he still felt a world of guilt and regret. He cursed his cowardice for not seeking help sooner.

He kissed his dad's cheek and wished him good night. His father took his hand and looked into his eyes. "Hello," he said, "Do I know you?" Tate reminded him one more time before he left that he was his son and promised to see him the next day. He thanked the attendant and let himself out, pausing outside the building to release the sob that he had been holding back for the past two hours. Christ. That had been the most difficult thing ever.

The hotel Dave had booked was only six blocks west of the nursing facility so Tate decided to walk. He strapped on his pack and headed west. The sidewalks weren't quite as crowded at this hour so he let his tears fall unchecked. He had to purge himself of some of the emotion that was building up inside or he'd burst. He thought of Alyson and wondered if Bernie had been able to reach her. He was so disappointed he hadn't been able to contact her and see her before he left. He was determined to go back but that might take weeks depending on how long it took to get his affairs in order here and get his documentation issued.

He laughed to himself when he reached the address Dave had given him. Of course it was an upscale hotel that probably cost a fortune. Dave had insisted on booking and paying but Tate would definitely pay him back. His check-in didn't pose any problem. The front desk clerk said they had been expecting him and they accepted his temporary identification without question. Undoubtedly that was Dave's handy work too.

His room was on the 50th floor and it was the most luxurious accommodations he had ever stayed in. Dave had really gone over the top. Whatever the hell his best friend was working at these days, it obviously paid well. The bed was presumably king sized but it looked massive. He figured it had to be custom made. There was a sitting area and from every angle of the corner room's floor to ceiling windows there were breathtaking views of the New York City skyline. It was amazing. The bathroom had an oversized Jacuzzi tub and his thoughts returned to Alyson. He would love to share this room with her. He wondered if it was too late to call her. With the time difference it would be after midnight in Newfoundland. He'd wait until tomorrow.

Tate grabbed a quick shower and tumbled into bed, exhausted. He fell into a deep, dreamless sleep and didn't stir until a persistent sound intruded on his slumber. He woke with a start realizing it was morning and the phone was ringing. He grabbed the bedside cordless and uttered a croaky hello into the receiver.

"Shit. I woke you didn't I?"

"Dave. Hey man. Are you here?"

"I am. My room is next door."

"Give me five minutes."

"I'll give you four," Dave said and laughed as he disconnected.

Tate shot out of bed, brushed his teeth and splashed water on his face. He shrugged on the jeans Alyson had bought him and one of the long sleeved tees just as a loud knock sounded on his door. He ran to open it and Dave rushed him the moment he did, wrapping him in a bear hug.

"God it's good to see you, man," Dave said, his voice gruff with emotion.

"You too, buddy. You too."

"Let me look at you," Dave said, stepping back. "Christ you haven't changed a bit. Fuck I don't think you've aged a day. How the hell did you manage that?"

"You haven't changed either. I'd know you anywhere." They stood at arms length, grasping each other's shoulders for long moments, just soaking in the moment and reveling in the knowledge that they had more time.

"You saw your dad?'

"Yeah. It nearly killed me. He looks so old. So weak."

"Time has really kicked his ass, Tate."

"It has. It's so difficult to see him like that."

"I'm assuming you want to go back this morning?"

"Yes I do. I have so much to do I don't know where to start."

"Let's go downstairs and grab a bite to eat. We'll make a list and I'll help you work through it. Okay?"

"Thanks Dave. I don't know what I'd do without you."

"It's what brothers do."

They hugged again and left the room, ready to tackle the myriad of logistics required for Tate to reestablish himself in his own life again.

CHAPTER 29

A week before Christmas Alyson was in the common room of the shelter, gathering mugs and plates that had not been returned to the kitchen wicket.

"You're still here, Princess," Nellie said in the snarky tone Alyson was coming to expect.

"I like you too much to leave, Nellie," she replied in good humour.

"Oh please. You'll find something better to do and we won't see your skinny ass back here again."

"You think my ass is skinny, Nellie? That's good. I thought I was putting on a few pounds."

"Oh piss off. You're too skinny and you know it."

"You're a fine one to talk, Miss Nellie. You could use a bit of extra meat on your bones."

"I'm the best kind the way I am, Princess."

"Do you have any plans for Christmas?"

"Don't you have a husband and kids? Someone else to torment besides me?"

"No I don't, Nellie. Just me. So how about it, any plans for Christmas?"

"None of your goddamn business that's not," Nellie grumbled but the sudden flash of sadness in her vivid blue eyes surprised Alyson. The old woman quickly blinked it away.

"No family in the area? Do you have someone to stay with?"

"Oh I got family girly but he doesn't want anything to do with a contrary old crow like me."

"Why is that?"

"None of your goddamn business."

"Fair enough. Can you at least tell me if you have somewhere to stay?"

"Why? You going to invite me home with you, Princess?"

"I don't want you out in the cold Nellie. Is there someone I can call?"

"Not that it's any of your business but I have a house. A fine house at that. Built in the late 1800s. It was grand in its day."

"I bet it was. So you're in out of the cold at night then?"

"I'm inside alright, Princess."

"Is your home heated?"

"What the hell do you think? Would I be coming here if I could afford heat?"

"Is there anything I can do to help?"

"I don't want your goddamn charity. Bad enough I got to scrounge up a meal here now and then."

"You said you had family. I could call them. They could help."

"Leave it alone girly. He's long given up on me."

"There are social workers that you can talk to. Do you want me to look into that for you?"

Nellie grunted and turned her head, signaling that the conversation was over. Alyson went back to the kitchen feeling disheartened. Sue and Lucy looked at her with peculiar expressions on their faces.

"What?" Alyson asked.

"That's the most that woman has said to anyone about her personal history in the last two years. She wouldn't even tell us that she had shelter. Well done." Sue squeezed her arm.

"Sounds like she doesn't have heat though and God knows the shape the house is in."

"You've got to learn to pick your battles, Alyson," Lucy said. "Most of these people have shelter but can't afford food and heat for their homes. We call them house poor folks. Some of them are truly homeless and couch surf, relying on the kindness of family and friends."

Alyson nodded and thought of Tate. He knew their plight. He had lived that harsh reality for so many years. She wondered yet again if any of the patrons had stories like his. Forgotten identities. Forgotten families. She contemplated following Nellie to see where she lived but with her luck, Nellie would have her arrested for stalking. Perhaps later she'd drive around some of the east end neighbourhoods where most of the historic homes were located and see if she could dig up some leads. Surely some businessperson in the area would know of Nellie. The rest of the shift passed in a blur of feeding the folks who wandered in throughout the afternoon, cleaning up the kitchen and replenishing the tea and coffee station in the common room. As Alyson said goodbye to the patrons, she couldn't help but notice that Nellie had left already. She was probably avoiding any further grilling.

Alyson drove along the east end streets, charmed by the towering poplar and maple trees that surrounded the grand houses. The homes had been built during a different time, in a different world. The architecture was breathtaking and the attention to detail and craftsmanship was truly inspired. The homes were rich with character and beauty. Houses like this simply weren't built any longer. Some of them were well maintained and looked to be in immaculate condition. Others were a little worn and weary looking, in need of love and a fresh coat of paint. Alyson was interested in the more run down homes that had been neglected over the years. Nellie was probably in one of those houses if the information she had provided was correct. Alyson saw a small corner store and pulled her car next to the curb.

A bell tinkled above her head as she entered the store. A woman in her sixties was behind the counter, dressed in a cotton floral dress with a bright red sweater primly buttoned. She wore faux-fur lined boots and the deep lines on her face suggested a two-pack a day habit. She smiled at Alyson and asked if she needed help with something. Alyson described Nellie and asked the shopkeeper if she knew her.

"Crotchety old bugger. Yes I know her," shop lady said with a chuckle, her throaty voice crackling with perpetual phlegm.

"Do you know where she lives? I'm concerned for her safety."

"Love if you show up on her doorstep she's likely to shoot you between the eyes," the woman warned.

"I'll take my chances," Alyson smiled.

The woman gave her directions to Nellie's house. She couldn't recall the street number but described the house in detail so Alyson wouldn't miss it. Alyson thanked her and before leaving picked up a loaf of bread, a jar of peanut butter, a container of whole milk and a bunch of bananas. If Nellie refused to see her, the least she could do was leave the food on her doorstep.

She made a couple of wrong turns but eventually found the small side street the shop lady had described and the faded blue house on the end had to be Nellie's place. She was right. It was grand. Or at least it had been in its heyday. Now it looked abandoned. There were no interior lights and Alyson wondered again if Nellie even had electricity. Maybe she simply hadn't returned home yet.

Taking a deep breath for courage, Alyson gathered up the paper shopping bags and cautiously made her way up the front walk. It wasn't shoveled but the track of fresh footprints indicated it had recently been used. She knocked on the door and waited several long moments. No one answered. She knocked again and waited, even calling Nellie's name. Again, no answer. Sighing and accepting defeat, she left the groceries on the front step and left. She drove around for a while and then went past the house again. The groceries were gone. Alyson smiled thinking at least the stubborn woman would have food in her belly tonight and tomorrow morning.

The next day at the shelter Nellie didn't show up. Alyson stressed that she had pushed too hard. She asked several of the regulars if they had seen her and they all said no. Nellie returned the day after but she wouldn't make eye contact with Alyson and ignored her completely when she said hello. Alyson was okay with that, but it made her even more determined to find out why she was estranged from her family. She decided to do a little digging when she got home that evening. She typed Nellie's address into her web browser. The house she lived in was a registered heritage building and the description of the house included a link to a secondary website that included an even more comprehensive history of the house. It also gave a history of the ownership of the house, including the current registered owner, Walter Howlett. *Gotcha, Nellie.*

A little more searching and Alyson uncovered the name of Nellie's purported estranged son, Nathan Walter Howlett. Apparently Walter had been Nellie's husband but she stumbled upon a death notice and his obituary dating back almost a decade. It was a little after eleven. Alyson wondered if it was too late to call Nathan Howlett. He was in Ontario so the one and a half hour time difference worked in her favour. She decided to take her chances, her hands shaking as she keyed in his telephone number.

Nellie was right. This really wasn't any of her business. Still, if she could help in any way it was worth running the risk of being told to mind her own business by the junior Howlett as well. Her heart was pounding as she listened to the ringing on the line. She was discouraged after four rings had gone unanswered but then a breathless hello from a deep male voice filled her ears.

"Hello. May I speak with Nathan Howlett please?" she was surprised by how nervous she sounded.

"This is Nate. May I ask who's calling?"

Alyson smirked; Nate had much better manners than his mother. "Hello, Mr. Howlett. My name is Alyson Fisher and I'm calling from Newfoundland. I work at a homeless shelter in downtown St. John's and I was wondering if you were aware that your mother is a regular there. I'm very concerned about her. I'm not sure if she has heat in her home or enough to eat when she's not visiting the shelter."

Her rushed statements were met with a long pause.

"Are you a social worker?"

"No. I'm a volunteer at the centre. I'm simply concerned for your mother's wellbeing and I wanted to reach out to you in case you weren't aware of her situation."

"Is she okay?"

"Yes. For now. But I can't imagine how she'll survive the winter in an unheated home."

"Does she know that you contacted me?"

"No. I did a little searching online and found you."

"What did she tell you about her situation?"

"Very little. She did say she had family but they wanted nothing to do with her."

"Well she has the part about family right. And I want to help her but she refuses to see me or accept any assistance. She fell apart after Dad died, started gambling and burned through her savings. I tried to get her help but she shut me out. Same with other extended family."

"I'm so sorry to hear that."

Nate drew in a ragged breath that Alyson felt in the pit of her stomach. She had a feeling he genuinely was not happy about the forced estrangement with his mother.

"Do you know how long she's been visiting the shelter?"

"I'm new there but one of the managers mentioned she's been a regular for about two years."

"Jesus," he said, his voice heavy with emotion.

"Is there any way you can visit? Perhaps reach out to her again?"

"Yes. But please don't tell her I'm coming or she'll disappear. Can you give me the address of the shelter?"

"Of course." Alyson provided the details and they exchanged cell phone numbers.

"Thank you for tracking me down, Alyson."

"My pleasure. If it was my mom, I'd want to know."

"Thanks again. Good night."

"Good night," Alyson disconnected the call and brushed away the tears that were trickling down her face. That had gone so much better than she had dared hope. She prayed that Nellie would give Nate a chance and accept his help.

She wearily turned off the downstairs lights, double checked the lock on the front door and dragged herself up the stairs to her bedroom. Her foot was hurting a little and she contemplated taking a hot bath but couldn't summon the energy. She stared across the hall at the spare bed and was hit broadside by a fresh wave of sadness. She missed Tate with every breath. Missed his handsome face. His quiet intellect. The way he filled her space. The way he filled her heart. Her mind. Her body.

He had called several times but she didn't answer her phone or listen to his voice messages. It was difficult to ignore him and thankfully the calls eventually stopped. She wondered how Vicki felt about him calling her. She probably wasn't thrilled, especially if Tate had shared the details of their relationship. She was aching to know how he was doing now that he had returned to his old life but she needed to keep the emotional distance in place to handle his sudden departure. She couldn't risk falling apart again.

Alyson was handling his absence opposite the way she had handled losing Joe. She threw herself into her volunteer work and when she was alone in the house it was never silent. She'd blast the stereo or leave the TV on for company. She avoided silence. She avoided any quiet time that would provide her opportunity to think. And remember. And wish for impossible things. She was still considering getting a puppy but she worried that the animal would be alone too much with her working at the shelter all day. She had bought a tree and decorated it with brightly coloured ornaments. She placed decorations throughout the house and forced herself to be merry, *dammit*. She set a frenetic pace that consumed every ounce of her time and energy so that she fell into bed exhausted at night and usually slept like the dead. As far as strategies went, it seemed to be working just fine. Of course, Tate was alive and well, so knowing that helped, too.

Alyson forced her thoughts back to Nate and Nellie. She couldn't imagine not being in contact with her family for such a long period of time. Granted her moving so far away from her own family wasn't much different than Nellie's choice to turn her back on her son. Alyson felt an overwhelming need to see her parents and Syd. And Lois. She was happy with her choice to move east but she wasn't happy with how she'd left things with her family and it was time to set things right again. She shuffled out to her office and opened her laptop. She impulsively decided that instead of couriering her gifts to her family, she would deliver them in person. She hastily booked a non-refundable ticket before she could change her mind. She was booked to fly out late on the 23rd, arriving in Vancouver midday on Christmas Eve. She belatedly thought of Sue, Lucy and the shelter. She had been scheduled to cover the Christmas Eve shift but she could remember Sue saying that finding volunteers during the holidays was never an issue. Many families had made volunteering at the shelter part of their own holiday traditions. She would call Sue first thing in the morning to let her know of her newly made plans.

    She started to close the cover on her laptop but hesitated. She looked through her browser history. The links were still there. The archived stories of Tate's appeal to the media to help him discover his identity were just a click away. She hovered her mouse over the first link and then quickly clicked. Oh God. That face. Those jade eyes. That clean-shaven square jaw. The dark, closely cropped hair. She would never forget how he looked leaning against her car after having his beard shaved off and his hair cut. She could close her eyes and still see the nervousness and anticipation in his eyes as he waited for her to recognize him. That had been the best day of her life.

    She shut down the laptop but instead of returning to her bedroom, she went to the spare room. She hesitated but then decided to allow herself this one indulgence. She crawled under the covers. She had changed the sheets weeks ago but somehow she could still sense him in the room. In the bed. She closed her eyes and summoned his image, praying she would dream of him, praying he would kiss her in her dreams. And hold her. And love her.

CHAPTER 30

Tate looked around the furnished two-bedroom condo he had just leased for the next six months. He had opted for a short-term lease because he was still uncertain if he would stay in the city or move somewhere else. Technically New York was home but it no longer felt like home. Especially not since his dad has passed away, just days after his return. They had so little time together but he spent the days they did have caring for his father and answering his questions over and over every few minutes while his dad was awake. He had been with him when he died. His father had been sleeping when Tate noticed a slight change in his breathing. It had gotten shallower and raspy. He pressed the call button and alerted the staff. A doctor dropped by and told Tate it would probably just be a matter of hours. In fact, his dad passed within the hour, with Tate holding his hand, telling him how much he was loved. He wished there had been more that he could have done. He simply had been too late. By more than a decade.

Dave stayed in New York for an additional week after the funeral. He had helped Tate with all of the arrangements. The funeral had been well attended by a large circle of friends and extended family wanting to pay their final respects and welcome Tate back. Vicki and her husband attended as well. Vicki was right. He had liked her husband even if seeing them together made him sad for the time he had missed. He wanted a wife. He wanted a family of his own. He didn't want to live a solitary life anymore. Everyone had been in awe of his story but truthfully he was tired of telling it. Tired of trying to figure out how to fit in a life that was foreign to him after his fifteen-year absence. He was tired, full stop. He missed Alyson. She was freezing him out and he wasn't sure why.

He was still waiting on his permanent passport. Dave had helped him with that too. He had more patience than Tate in dealing with government departments that complicated the hell out of everything with layers of bureaucracy. Tate was so sick of filling out forms and standing in long lines that never seemed to move. Even though he knew who he was, he had never felt so lost. Part of it was losing his dad so soon after finding him and of course part of it was missing Alyson with every breath. He thanked the universe again for Dave's support during the first two weeks of his return. He had felt guilty for keeping him from his family for so long but his presence had gotten him through the rough patches.

Dave had also been there for his parents while he had been missing. He stepped in and advised them on investments and when Tate's father realized his mental health was failing, he signed over his power of attorney to Dave. It had been incredibly practical and forward thinking of his dad, despite his diminishing mental capacity. Dave had looked after securing him a placement at the long-term care facility when he could no longer take care of himself. It was one of the best in the state. It hadn't been cheap but Dave helped Tate's father invest his savings and then when it came time to sell his condo, Dave had fetched top dollar and invested that as well.

Tate had cried when he read his father's will. His entire estate had been bequeathed to him. Dave told Tate that both of his parents had been hopeful that he was still alive. The will stipulated that the estate was to be held in trust for ten years after his father's passing. If Tate still hadn't been located in that time period, the funds were to be released to a charity of Dave's choice. Tate had been staggered to see the sum of money that had accumulated over the past fifteen years. He owed Dave so much for all he had done for his family. All that he had done for him. He was incredibly blessed to have a friend like him.

He had called Alyson's home and cell numbers several times over the past weeks but she never answered and didn't reply to his messages. He was surprised and hurt that she would turn her back on him so completely. He had a momentary pang of alarm that perhaps something bad had happened to her and contacted Bernie to check on her. When Bernie let him know that she was well but busy he decided to back off. For now. He was told that it might take weeks for his passport application to process. He felt frustrated and helpless but for the time being he was stuck and there wasn't a damn thing he could do about it except wait it out.

Dave wanted him to spend Christmas with his family in Seattle. He was thinking about it but would rather spend it with Alyson in Newfoundland. That was impossible without his passport. He thought about the frame he had bought for her. He hadn't had time to work on the sketch he wanted to give her for Christmas. Until now. He went to the spare bedroom and dug through the lone box on the bed containing most of the items that had been in his pack. He found his sketchpad and pencils and brought them to the living room. The view from his window was of the building across the street, more condos, more people in boxes. It was nothing like the view of the ocean from Alyson's living room window. He reclined on the couch and drew up his knees, resting the sketchbook against his thighs. The leather was stiff and not nearly as comfortable as Alyson's couch. He selected a soft black pencil and started sketching, the details filling in quickly as he recreated the scene that was ineradicably etched in his memory. As the picture came to life beneath his skilled fingers, he smiled, hoping she would like it. He added the final touches, signed the print and then placed it in the frame. It turned out even better than he had hoped. Now he just had to send it to her and pray that it broke through the wall she had erected between them.

CHAPTER 31

Alyson was checking the coffee cart in the common room when a well-dressed man in his late forties walked into the room. He was short and trim with thinning hair and vivid blue eyes. She had seen those eyes before. *Holy crap. This must be Nathan Howlett.* She glanced around the room quickly to confirm that Nellie had not arrived yet. She hurried over to the stranger.

"Mr. Howlett?" she asked, smiling.

He extended his hand, "Hi. Please call me Nate. You must be Alyson."

"Yes I am. It's very nice to meet you, Nate. I'm so happy that you were able to come."

"Is Mom here?"

"No but she's usually here by noon. We have a quiet room where you can wait if you'd like."

"Thank you. I'd appreciate that. I have to gather up my wits to do battle with her," he chuckled.

"Yes. She's feisty."

Nate laughed, "That's one word for it."

Alyson led him to a small room at the end of a long hallway past the kitchen. The space was a multi-purpose room used by the visiting social worker and nurses who stopped by weekly. Sometimes the patrons slipped away in there to use the phone and talk to relatives. It was empty now and Alyson invited Nate to take a seat.

"Would you like something to drink?"

"Do you have hard liquor?" he quipped.

She smiled, "Sorry. Best I can do is coffee, tea or water."

"Black coffee would be great."

"I'll be right back," Alyson smiled at Nellie's son and headed back to the kitchen to get his coffee. She peeked into the common room and was surprised to see that Nellie had arrived. She hurried back to the quiet room and set Nate's mug on the table.

"She's here," Alyson said, breathless and anxious now that the moment had come for Nellie to be reunited with her son.

"Oh God. Already. How do we do this?" Nate asked, also clearly shaken.

"I'll lie. I'll tell her that the nurse is back here and wants to check her vitals. She might resist. She usually does."

"You're devious. I'm willing to bet my mother likes you."

Alyson grinned, "If she does, she hides it well. Okay. Wish me luck. And good luck to you. I have a feeling she's not going to be very happy with either one of us."

"Thank you Alyson. I appreciate all that you've done."

"My pleasure, Nate."

Alyson returned to the common room. Nellie had already pulled off the green scarf and gloves and was shrugging out of her jacket when Alyson stopped in front of her.

"What the heck do you want now, Princess?" Nellie asked, looking old and frail despite her bravado.

"The nurse is back in the quiet room, Miss Nellie. She wants to check your blood pressure."

"Oh tell her to bugger off. My pressure is the best kind."

"Come on Nellie. Do it to shut me up. I'll keep bugging you."

"My God you're such a nuisance. Leave me alone and go cook my lunch."

"Nellie it will take five minutes of your time to visit with the nurse. Or you can argue with me for the rest of the day."

Nellie muttered something under her breath and stood with a huff, taking her coat, scarf and gloves with her.

"I can hold on to those for you," Alyson offered.

"You'll do no such thing, you bully. I'm going to see your stupid nurse so go on. Leave me alone."

"Okay, Nellie. Have it your way," Alyson said, standing in the hallway and watching her slowly move toward the room where her son waited. She swallowed a moment of panic, wondering how Nellie would react to seeing her son.

She heard Nellie say, "What the hell?" before the door closed. It was up to Nate now. She didn't envy him the battle that was about to unfold.

She returned to the kitchen and checked on the lasagnas in the oven. The other volunteers were busy setting out plates, cutting up bread and doing the hundreds of little things that came automatically to them. She kept one eye on the clock while she tossed salads and filled sugar bowls and milk jugs. Nate and Nellie had been in the room for over thirty minutes. She prayed that was a good sign. She hadn't told anyone at the shelter what she had done or given any indication about what was happening back in the quiet room. If it backfired, she didn't want to take anyone down with her; she'd suffer the wrath of Nellie on her own.

She was cutting one of the lasagnas when she saw Nate and Nellie walk by the kitchen door. She put down the knife and rushed out after them.

"Nellie. Everything okay?" she asked, glancing between the tiny woman and her son.

"You. Don't you speak to me. You are a busy body. That's what you are, Princess. Sticking your nose in where it don't belong."

"Mom. That's enough. Alyson was trying to help you. I'm happy she called me."

Nellie tossed her head and grunted, muttering away under her breath. Nate turned to Alyson while Nellie shrugged on her jacket.

"Mom has agreed to come home with me for Christmas. We'll figure things out during her visit."

"That's wonderful! Nellie I hope you'll have a wonderful Christmas."

Again Nellie grunted, but when Alyson caught her eye she could tell she had been crying and the hardness she usually saw in her face was gone. Alyson fought back tears as Nate hugged her, thanking her again for reaching out to him.

"Merry Christmas to you both," Alyson said, respecting Nellie's pride even though she was aching to hug the cantankerous old woman. She walked them out and waved goodbye from the bottom step as Nate escorted his mother to his rental car. She had just turned to go back inside when she heard Nellie's raspy voice call out, "Princess."

She turned, "Yes, Nellie?"

"Merry Christmas to you too. And for the love of God, eat something. No man is gonna want you if you're all skin and bones."

"Thanks, Nellie. I will," she smiled. She gave a final wave and went back inside, wondering what Nate had said to convince his mother to go back to Ontario with him.

"What was that all about? Who was that man with Nellie?" Lucy asked when Alyson stepped back into the warmth of the building. Alyson quickly filled her in as they walked back to the kitchen.

"You're a brave woman, Alyson Fisher."

"Or a foolish one. I hope it works out."

Any further discussion was preempted by the organized chaos of serving lunch to the dozens of folks waiting in the common room. They usually saw their biggest crowds on the colder days. The shelter was an escape for many from the elements. Even those who were couch surfing didn't want to be underfoot in someone else's home all day. Alyson's smile was genuine as she plated the food, letting her mind drift to both Nellie and Tate. Both of them were warm and safe. She was grateful for that.

She went straight home after her shift, anxious to start packing for her flight to Vancouver later that night. She decided not to tell anyone in her family she was flying home. She did let Lois in on her surprise and her friend happily agreed to pick her up at the airport when she arrived the next day. Alyson was just heading up the stairs when her doorbell rang. Whenever there was someone at the door a part of her always hoped it might be Tate. That was impossible but her foolish heart continued to dream despite her best efforts to move on and get over him.

It was a courier with a package for her. She signed for it, her eyes drawn to the return address. New York. *Oh God. It was probably from Tate.* She mumbled a thank you to the courier, closed the front door and walked to the kitchen, pulling herself up on one of the island stools. He had sent her something. Her hands were shaking as she turned the package over and over in her hands. It was a standard courier box. She pulled on the perforated tab and peeked inside. There was a flat object wrapped in layers of bubble wrap. With shaking hands, she removed the layers of plastic to reveal a wrapped gift with a card taped to the front. She opened the card first. It was a simple note card with a sprig of holly on the front and on the inside, Tate had scribbled,

I miss you. Love, Tate

Love, Tate. She read those two words over and over again. *I miss you.* Oh God, Tate. I miss you, too. She took a deep breath and forced herself to remember he was married. He was taken.

She had to focus on that. She considered not opening the gift but her curiosity was driving her mad. She pulled off the red ribbon and tore away the festive gift wrap. She gasped. It was a framed print. He had sketched them. He had perfectly captured him carrying her in his arms through the snowy forest. Her bright red hat was the only splash of colour in the otherwise black and white print. It was perfect. Alyson started to sob. Right or wrong, she longed to be back in his arms again.

She walked to the pantry and pulled out a bottle of her favourite merlot. She twisted off the cap and reached into a cabinet to pull out a glass. The fragrant scent of the wine enveloped her. God it would be so simple to fill the glass. To chug it back and numb the pain. She was flying out in six hours. She didn't want to compound a long travel day with a hangover. She closed her eyes and let the sadness and loneliness wash over her. This was the risk of loving, of letting someone get close. When they left, you hurt. But she would survive it. She wouldn't have changed the time with Tate, not for anything, so she had to accept the pain now.

She capped the wine and placed it back in the pantry. She picked up the beautifully carved frame and looked at the print again. She paused. There was something familiar about the frame that she couldn't put her finger on. She was certain she hadn't seen it before. Oh God! The etchings on the frame were of Celtic knots, identical to those on the cover of the journal she bought for him. What were the chances? She walked to the living room, stopping to look around the space. She decided to place the print on the mantle so she could see it every time she walked by.

She was amazed by his talent. He was gifted. He had sketched them from behind so their faces weren't showing. She could remember how fascinated she had been with his green eyes. How he wouldn't hold her gaze. He had told her that he avoided people, yet he hadn't hesitated to carry her through the forest, comfort her when she cried, tend to her every need. The sketch brought it all back. She pulled the blanket off the couch and curled up on what she had come to consider his spot. She started the fireplace and stared at the print, allowing herself the extravagance of reliving every moment they had spent together. She knew she had to move forward, and she would. But for now she wanted to remember how it had felt getting to know him, watching his walls crumble and witnessing his return to the living. Now she wanted to immerse herself in the memory of his warmth when he saved her from the blizzard, when he held her in his arms and kissed her, when he made love to her. Her body instantly responded to the remembered passion they had shared. She closed her eyes and let all of the memories consume her.

CHAPTER 32

"Uncle Tate! Uncle Tate! It's Christmas morning! You gotta get up so we can open our presents!"

Dave's daughter, Ireland, a precocious six year old who had Tate wrapped around her little finger, was tugging on his arm, rousing him from a sweet dream about Alyson.

"Okay, Squirt. I'm getting up. Just give me a minute, okay?"

"Okay but you have to hurry so I'll give you half a minute," she commanded over her shoulder as she raced back into the living room.

Tate roared with laughter. He wanted a child just like her one day. Soon. She was a hoot. Dave's older daughter Joy was eleven but thought she was twenty and he didn't envy Dave and Zara their daily battles with her over the simplest of things. Their son Tate was twelve and was more reserved. Tate had been touched when he learned Dave had named his son after him. The young man had warmed a little to Tate since he arrived and couldn't believe his uncle hadn't played a video game in more than fifteen years. Despite his best efforts to keep up, his namesake repeatedly kicked his ass during their epic screen battles.

Tate stretched and let his thoughts drift to Alyson, inevitably as they always did. He conjured up her beautiful face and was wondering if she was alone this morning when Ireland's shrill little voice cut through the house.

"Uncle Tate. Time is up. Come on already."

Tate laughed again as he heard both Zara and Dave tell her to use her manners and lower her voice. He quickly used the bathroom, brushed his teeth and hastened to the living room.

"You can sit by me," Ireland declared and Tate lowered himself onto the couch next to the commander and chief.

Zara handed him a cup of coffee, "Reinforcements," she smiled.

"Thanks," he took a long sip. "So good." It wasn't as good as Alyson's coffee though. He mentally smiled as she slipped into his thoughts yet again.

Dave played Santa and handed out the gifts. Tate was surprised and touched to see there were several gifts for him. He had enjoyed buying gifts for all of them too even though it had been challenging figuring out what to get the kids. Zara had helped him with his list. He was especially excited for Dave to open his gift. Tate had given him premium seat tickets to the Super Bowl. It was the least he could do after all Dave had done for him and his parents.

He enjoyed watching the kids open their gifts. Ireland was excited over everything, and even Joy and young Tate let their true selves shine through as they got caught up in the festive spirit of the morning. Tate was so grateful to share this morning with them. He caught Dave looking at him several times, shaking his head in disbelief, his eyes glossy with tears. Tate felt pretty much the same way.

Later that morning while the kids were occupied with their gifts and Zara was on the phone with her parents in Texas, Dave and Tate retreated to the relative quiet of the downstairs family room for a break before the chaos of dinner preparations started.

"Any word from your friend, Alyson?" Dave asked.

"No. She hasn't returned any of my calls or messages," Tate sighed, his frustration running over.

"Try her today. It's Christmas. Everyone is feeling more generous at Christmas."

"Yeah. Maybe."

"What's the story with you two? You've been very skilled at evading the subject whenever I bring it up."

Tate pushed his fingers through his hair, wondering how he could possibly explain to anyone how deeply he felt for Alyson despite the short time they had spent together.

"I'm in love with her. And given her complete withdrawal since I left, I'm pretty sure she doesn't feel the same way."

"Wow. Man that's a tough one. You fell in love with her? That soon?"

"How long were you with Zara before you fell in love?"

"Good point. I knew pretty much from the first time I kissed her that she was for me."

"Well there you go. That's how I felt with Alyson too. Even before we kissed."

"Call her, Tate. If you love her and want to be with her, don't give up. Find out why she's not returning your calls."

"You're right. I'll try her number."

"Use my upstairs study. It's quiet and off-limits to Miss Ireland. She is really going to miss you when you leave tomorrow. We all will."

"I'm going to miss you guys too. But now that I'm back in the land of the living, you'll be sick of seeing me."

"You can give that your best shot. I still can't quite believe you're here. I can't even tell you, Tate, how grateful I am that you're alive."

"I'm pretty grateful to have my life back. I just have to figure out what to do with it moving forward."

"Go make that call. I have a feeling it's your first step. I'll distract Ireland when we go back to the first floor so you can escape to the study."

"Thanks man," Tate gave Dave a quick hug as they stood and started up the stairs from the basement level. Tate waited on the top step until he heard Dave ask Ireland to show him one of her new toys before he quickly rounded the corner and continued up the next flight of stairs to the third floor. He went to the window of Dave's study and looked out over Seattle harbour as he hit the speed dial for Alyson's landline. The phone rang unanswered until her voice mail cut in. He almost hung up but last minute decided to leave a message.

"Merry Christmas, Alyson. I was hoping to catch you at home. I hope you are well. I miss you. Please call me back."

He disconnected and pressed his head against the cool window pane feeling disheartened and lonely. He tried her cell number but it went straight to voice mail. She was either on a call or it was turned off. He waited several minutes, redialed but got her voice mail again. Dammit. He prayed that his passport was processed soon so he could book a flight back to Newfoundland and see her in person. He had to know what was going on in that beautiful head of hers.

Perhaps she had simply been caught up in the drama of their scare in the storm and he was merely a warm body for her to seek temporary comfort. Perhaps she wasn't interested in him as a potential lover or boyfriend. Or husband. Perhaps she didn't want him at all. He closed his eyes and remembered how shattered he had felt after he had kissed her for the first time. It had been a stunning moment of clarity for him. He had no idea who he was or what his past held but he knew in that moment that he wanted his future to be with this woman. The days they shared had been the best of his life. Now that he could remember his past he knew with certainty that he had never known joy like he had experienced with Alyson. He and Vicki had been too young to even know what they wanted in their relationship and their marriage had been a disaster from the start.

He thought about the fifteen years of his life he had missed. He had lost count of the number of days he had gone hungry. The nights he had shivered from the cold in his tent. He thought of the times sickness had found him and he had felt so miserable that he almost wished to die. Almost. He regretted the time he would never get back with his parents and with Dave. But that convoluted and unlikely path, as long and brutal as it had been, had ultimately led him to Alyson.

He tried her number again but it still went to voice mail. Her phone must be off. He could hear Ireland calling his name. He was actually surprised that Dave had been able to distract her for this long. She had been his shadow since he arrived. He forced himself back to the present. He wanted to enjoy every moment of this day with his best friend and his incredible family. He couldn't do that if he continued to brood over Alyson. He sent a wish out to the universe that she was safe, happy and surrounded by people she loved, and left the sanctuary of Dave's study.

"Ireland! Where are you?" he called.

"I'm here, Uncle Tate. Where the heck did you go? I looked everywhere for you," she declared, launching herself into his arms.

Tate pressed a kiss against her sweet smelling hair. "I had to make a phone call so I used your dad's study."

"Oh. I'm not allowed in there. I accidentally coloured on some of daddy's important papers and he wasn't too happy about that."

Tate chuckled, "I bet he wasn't, Squirt."

"Nope. Can we play dress up now? I want to be a superhero and you can be the princess. Okay?"

"You betcha. Do I get a tiara?"

"Yup. It's shiny."

"Then I'm a very lucky princess," Tate said as he lowered himself to the floor in the living room and let his six year old honorary niece wrap a bright pink feather boa around his neck and ceremoniously place a gaudy plastic crown on his head.

"Mom can I borrow your lipstick please?" Ireland yelled loud enough for her mother to hear her wherever she might be in the house. Joy who was sitting on the sofa playing with her new phone snickered at the prospect of Tate getting an actual makeover.

Tate laughed as Zara called from the kitchen, "No you may not. Uncle Tate is beautiful without makeup."

Tate would miss Ireland. And Dave. All of them. He had enjoyed his week in Seattle with Dave and his family but he was booked to fly back to New York early the next morning. He didn't want to outstay his welcome. Plus he was anxious to check on the status of his passport. He already had his driver's license and social security reinstated. He just needed his passport, his key to returning to Alyson. He also had to tackle the mundane chores of getting health coverage, buying a car, looking for a job. He was seriously considering painting full time. He could afford to do that. Simply create and see if there was a receptive market for his offerings. Maybe he'd give himself a year to do just that and if it didn't fly, he'd try something else. He had dabbled in oil painting as a teenager but never had the time, or interest back then, to focus on his art. Since creating that simple sketch for Alyson, he felt a yearning to create more.

"I declare you're the prettiest princess I've ever seen," Ireland said, her sweet little arms winding around his neck. Tate belatedly realized that she had gotten into her mother's makeup. She passed him a small mirror so he could see for himself. He roared laughing at the fire engine red lipstick that not only covered his lips but an inch wide perimeter around his mouth as well and the blue eyeshadow that circled his eyes was indescribable. He heard a click and then snorts of laughter as Dave captured the moment in perpetuity on his phone's camera.

"I am posting this online," he chuckled as he dodged out of Tate's grasp.

"Not on your life, Dave," Tate said as he and Ireland playfully chased him from the room.

A few hours later as Tate sat down in front of the bountiful feast prepared by Zara and Dave, most of the makeup scrubbed from his face though his mouth was stained unnaturally red, he felt thankful to be surrounded by love and laughter. It wasn't quite the Christmas that he had envisioned. Alyson wasn't by his side. But it was a pretty close second.

CHAPTER 33

"Come on, Al," Sydney called from the living room of their parent's condo. "All of the good stuff is going to be gone."

"I can't believe you've talked me into shopping for Boxing Day deals. The malls are going to be madhouses," Alyson grumbled, buttoning her blouse as she walked into the room.

"Suck it up, Sis. It'll be fun. We haven't done this in forever. Ready?"

"God help me. I think so. Mom sure you won't come with us? Dad's at the office. You'll be all alone."

Lily Mathews shook her head in vigorous refusal of the offer. "You girls are far braver than me. Go and enjoy. I'm going to meet your Dad at the park for a hike later."

"The park sounds nice. Come on Syd. Let's go to the park with Mom and Dad instead."

"No. I need a dress for a New Year's Eve date and you have to help me."

"Who's the date?"

"Just some guy I've been seeing."

"He must be special if you're willing to go shopping Christmas week." Alyson groaned in surrender, "Okay. Let's get this over with."

"That's the spirit, Al. Bye Mom."

Alyson kissed their mom goodbye and followed her sister out of the condo. She smiled when Syd linked arms with her and confessed, "I selfishly wanted you to myself for a couple of hours, Al. We don't have to go to the mall. We can do whatever you want."

Alyson squeezed her sister's hand. "Tell you what, let's give ourselves one hour at the mall. We'll hit the high-end dress stores and find you something fabulous. But then I want to go to the rink and ice skate for a while. Deal?"

"Oh that would be fun! We'll have to rent skates."

"That's fine. But first let's find you a dress to knock the socks off this new beau of yours."

"He's not really my beau. And I'm aiming to knock his pants off so we're going to have to outdo ourselves on the dress."

Alyson laughed at her sister's bawdiness. She had always been the more outspoken and over the top one. Some things never changed. Syd and her parents had been so surprised when she rang the doorbell of her parents' condo mid-afternoon on Christmas Eve. Everyone had actually started crying, including Alyson and Lois who had been smiling like the Cheshire cat since meeting her at the airport. It was pure coincidence that Syd had even been there at that time. She had stopped by to drop off a couple of things in preparation for the celebration the next day. She had been intending to go back to her own condo but decided to spend the night after Alyson arrived. It had been fun and reminded Alyson of the Christmases of her youth and teenage years. It had felt good to make her family so happy and she apologized to all of them for her withdrawal over the past couple of years. Even though she knew she had hurt them, repeatedly, they were quick to allay her concerns and insisted apologies weren't necessary. Regardless, Alyson was intent on making it up to them with more visits and letting them back into her life.

"Earth to Al. Hello. Anyone home?"

"Sorry. I was thinking about Christmas Eve."

"You surprised the hell out of everyone. Best Christmas in a long time though. I'm so happy you changed your mind and came home."

Alyson wrapped her arm around her sister, "Me too."

They walked through the underground parking garage and as soon as they were settled inside the car, Sydney casually brought up Tate. Alyson was actually surprised it had taken her that long.

"Are you still in touch with Tate?"

"No. He's called and left a couple of messages but I haven't answered or returned them."

"Why not?"

"He's married. I don't belong in his remembered life."

"But you were just friends, weren't you? That's what you told us."

Alyson twisted her hands in her lap but remained silent.

"Jesus, Al. Did you sleep with the homeless dude?"

"I don't want to talk about it."

"Holy shit! You did! What was he like? I bet he was wild."

"That's enough Sydney. Stop it."

"Fuck me! You fell for that dude. Seriously?"

"Don't be ridiculous. We were just friends."

"Then why are you turning purple and why are your hands shaking?"

"Keep your eyes on the road, Syd."

"Al are you okay? Seriously?"

"Yes. I'm okay."

"But you miss him?" Syd asked softly.

Alyson hesitated but then admitted the truth, "Yes. I miss him. And yes I have feelings for him."

"Wow. That's heavy, Sis."

"I know."

"He's been gone for fifteen years. Maybe he can't pick things up where they left off with his wife. She thought he had died. Maybe she moved on. Did you think about that?"

"You didn't see her, Syd. She was so happy to see him. She was in disbelief. And he knew her instantly."

Silence filled the car. Sydney waited several moments before speaking.

"My date for the party this weekend has a single friend. I've met him. He's an investment banker but don't hold that against him. He's really nice, Al. I think you'd like him. And he would adore you. I could make a call."

"Thanks but no thanks. I'll probably go back to Newfoundland before the weekend."

"I was hoping you'd stay."

"I've enjoyed being back in Vancouver, and spending time with you, Mom and Dad. But Newfoundland is my home now and I'd like to get back. I'm missing the shelter and the folks there."

"They'd understand if you took a few more days. I've missed you so much. This is the first time you've seemed like yourself since Joe died. I love having you back, Sis."

"I'm sorry I pushed you away, Syd. I didn't do it to be mean or hurtful. I just couldn't cope with everything."

"I know. And please stop apologizing. I understand that you felt you had to run away."

"Yes. I suppose I did."

"And is going back to Newfoundland instead of going on a date running away too?"

"No it isn't. I'm making a life there. I'm making friends there."

"Really? Who do you hang out with besides the people at the shelter?"

"Before I came here I dropped in on my nearest neighbours with a tray of Christmas cookies. The woman, Amanda, is around my age and her husband seems a little older. They have two young kids. Amanda and I have made a tentative date for coffee. I got a really good vibe from her."

"Okay, that's a good start. But you have to promise me that you won't spend all of your time alone in that big house. Please make friends. Join a gym. Do social things. Okay?"

"I promise. Syd I thought I was going to die in the woods that day. It was the ultimate wake up call. I am grateful Tate came back and found me and got us both safely back to the house. The blizzard came up so fast. We both could have perished."

"I hope some day I can meet him so I can thank him for saving my big sister."

"I don't think that's likely but I love you for wanting to do that. Oh. There's the mall. Let the craziness begin."

"God now that we're here I don't want to go in. There's no where to park."

"We'll be in and out in an hour. And then we skate."

Sydney saw a parking spot open up and deftly pulled her compact VW into the vacated space.

"Let's shop!" she said, grabbing her purse and squaring her shoulders as they joined the throngs of other bargain-hungry people heading into the mall. Alyson decided she'd buy a dress too. She and Lois had made plans to paint the town red before she left. While her heart wasn't completely into it, she was determined to plaster on a happy face and make the most of a night out with her best friend. She knew it would be fun. Lois made everything fun. She planned to consume large amounts of alcohol too. Perhaps she'd even open herself up to the possibility of flirting with someone new.

Tate flashed across her thoughts.

Okay, maybe she wasn't quite ready for flirting yet. Baby steps still meant progress. Slowly but surely.

CHAPTER 34

Tate reached for his sunglasses as he emerged from the subway on Fulton Street in lower Manhattan. The sunshine seemed especially bright after the artificial lighting of the underground. He unzipped his jacket, enjoying the unseasonably high temperatures for mid-January. He inhaled deeply, smiling at the remembered familiarity of the scents that were distinctively New York; exhaust, concrete, food vendors and a healthy dash of humanity. The bright blue sky reminded him of the blue-eyed woman he had left behind in Newfoundland. With considerable effort, he pushed Alyson to the back of his mind. He walked along thinking of what he had to do today. What he had wanted to do since remembering and returning.

He seamlessly merged with the throng of people walking along the crowded sidewalks, the smooth undulating flow of the masses occasionally interrupted by a tourist stopping to take a picture. Tate kept his gaze trained on the tall building ahead, glancing up at the spire now and then. It was beautiful and as an architect he fully appreciated the complexity and artistry of the design. The One World Trade Centre stood tall and distinctive near the site of the original towers. He swallowed back tears as he approached the entrance and paused for a moment to soak up the impact of the building.

He continued along Fulton Street, casting an occasional glance over his shoulder at the Trade Centre. As much as he wanted to tour the building, it wasn't his destination today. He turned onto Greenwich and felt his heart race as he approached the 9/11 Memorial. He had seen photos of the memorial site online but the reality of the twin reflecting pools built on the footprints of the original towers was something you really couldn't prepare for in advance. Tate went to the monument pool built on the base of the north tower. He knew his own name wouldn't be etched in the brass plates surrounding the exterior walls of the pools. His parents had been so certain he was alive, despite the overwhelming evidence that suggested otherwise. He was grateful now that his parents had so fervently believed he had not died in the attack. Yet, Tate knew several people who had died and he slowly moved around the north pool, reading the names of those who had not survived the events of that horrific day. He wasn't sure how much time had passed until he found the names he was looking for; the two men and three women he had been supposed to meet with that morning. Kyle. Geneviève. Deborah. Tomas. Elena. He traced each of their names with his fingers, oblivious to the tears running down his face. He barely knew them but that was irrelevant. He was shedding tears for each and every name etched on the plaques. He wasn't the only one. A woman a few feet away caught his eye and wiping away tears, she smiled at him kindly. He smiled back, appreciating their unspoken camaraderie.

Tate walked to the south tower pool and read every name on the plates there too. He wondered about their stories. Were they mothers and fathers? Lovers and friends? Children and siblings? What plans had they left unfinished? What goodbyes were left unsaid? How many dreams crumbled in the rubble of the towers that day? Too many to count. Too many to comprehend. He closed his eyes for a moment and focused on the soothing flow of the cascading waters over the interior walls of the pool. It was peaceful and serene. It was a beautiful monument.

He wandered away from the pools and walked among the trees that had been planted as part of the memorial plaza. Again, he felt at peace. He sought out a vacant bench and sat, facing the pools, watching the people as they came to remember and reflect. A missed train and an irate wife had saved his life that morning. He could remember feeling irritated that he would be late for his meeting. He had been about to close the deal on a design for low cost, energy efficient housing to help combat the growing problem of homelessness in his city and country. And then Vicki had called and completely derailed his morning. And saved his life. If he had caught the early train that day, his name would be etched in bronze too.

He turned his face toward the sun and sent a prayer of gratitude for being spared that day and his subsequent return to life. He thought about the housing project. He liked the idea of contributing in some small way to reducing homelessness, even more so now that he had lived it himself for so long. Dave had kept all of his things in storage, knowing it's what his parents would have wanted. Perhaps he'd dig out those plans and revisit the idea. It was time to sift through that storage unit and figure out what pieces of his old life he needed to keep. It was definitely time to move on.

Homes for the homeless. Yeah. That seemed like a good place to start.

CHAPTER 35

Alyson yawned as she drove along the rutted, winding road that lead to her driveway. The alternating deep freezes and thaws of January were wrecking havoc on the roads, creating dips and ruts and potholes unlike anything she had previously experienced. The shelter had been busy today, but despite the hustle, she missed crotchety Nellie. Her son had called a couple of weeks ago to let her know his mom would be staying with him for the winter months and they were hoping to find a smaller, more affordable home for her to move into back in St. John's in the spring. Alyson was relieved everything had worked out for Nellie and her son. She looked forward to visiting her when she settled in her new place, whether the grumpy old woman liked it or not.

She pulled into her driveway and was startled to see a car parked next to her house. She was considering backing up and calling the police when the driver's door opened and a man stepped out. Not just any man. It was Tate. Oh God. He was here. She started to tremble as she slowly pulled in next to his rental and shut off her car. She sat there for a moment just looking at him. He was alone. No Vicki. *Damn, he looked good.* He was clean-shaven and his hair was clipped short on the sides and slightly longer on top. It suited him. He was wearing the coat she had bought for him. His bright green eyes were boring into her as though trying to gauge her thoughts. Taking a deep breath for courage, she got out of her car, resisting the urge to run to him.

"Hi Tate," she said, her smile genuine. "It feels odd calling you that."

"Alyson. God it's good to see you," his voice was hoarse with emotion.

He closed the distance between them and pulled her into his arms. She returned his hug, relishing the solid feel of him, his intoxicating scent. She wanted to fade into him but Vicki's beautiful face flashed in her mind. She quickly pulled away and took a step back. He looked at her oddly.

"You didn't return my calls," he said.

"I'm sorry. I've been busy. I've been working."

"Too busy for a quick phone call?"

"I'm sorry, Tate."

Tate stared at her for several moments. Alyson realized she was holding her breath. When she didn't say anything else, he finally broke the awkward silence, his voice stiff but polite, "Where are you working?"

"Actually I'm volunteering at a homeless shelter."

"A shelter? That's pretty awesome," he smiled, his eyes holding hers, his wariness evident.

"Yeah, I really enjoy it. But enough about that, I want to hear about you. What brings you back here? How has it been settling back into your old life?"

"Are you going to invite me in?"

"Sorry. Yes. Of course." She led the way to the front door and unlocked it. "Would you like coffee? Are you hungry? I ate at the shelter but I can make you something," she offered as they kicked off their boots in the front hallway.

"Maybe later," he said, following her into the kitchen and leaning against the island as he watched her remove her coat and drape it over a bar stool. He shrugged out of his and placed it on top of hers.

"Let's go to the living room," she suggested, passing by him to sit on the far end of the sofa. She was shaking. This had been the last thing she had expected today. She honestly thought she would never see him again but now that he was here, she realized the progress she thought she had made in moving on was a joke. She wanted him so desperately, she ached.

He followed her into the room and sat next to her. She wasn't sure if she could think clearly with him so close to her. She noticed him looking at the print he had sent her, now displayed on the mantle.

"Thank you for that," she said. "It's beautiful."

"I'm happy you liked it. Those moments in the forest changed my life."

"Mine too. I would have died if you hadn't come back to save me."

"Thank God I heard you," he smiled, brushing her hair back behind her ear. Alyson shivered at the contact. She had to pull herself together.

"Please, Tate. I'm so anxious to hear all about you," she prodded, breaking the spell.

"I'm not sure where to even begin. So much has happened in my life without me. Vicki told me that my mom passed away. And my dad had advanced Alzheimer's."

Alyson gasped and reached out to squeeze his hand. "I'm so sorry. That must be very difficult for you to process." He wrapped her hand in both of his and Alyson longed to have the right to offer him the deeper comfort of an embrace.

"It was. It still is. I saw Dad a couple of days after I left here. He didn't know me and he died a few days later," Tate said, his eyes filling with tears as his hands clasped hers.

Alyson reluctantly pulled her hand away and wiped tears from her eyes, "I'm so deeply sorry to hear that. I can't even imagine how painful that must have been."

"Thank you, Alyson. It's been a difficult few weeks. Losing Dad was the worst of it though. He was so frail when I saw him that I wasn't really surprised. I'm grateful that I got to see him at all. Sadly I didn't have that chance with my mom."

"So she passed away a while ago?" Again she fought the impulse to physically comfort him with a touch. She couldn't believe he was here, sitting next to her. God she had missed him so much. Right or wrong, she missed him.

"Yes. Back in 2005. Vicki told me that Mom and Dad never stopped believing that I was alive. How I wish I had found my way back sooner to prove them right."

"I wish it had worked out that way for you too."

"My best friend Dave met up with me in New York and helped me get things in order. I now have a driver's license and a passport. I exist again."

"I'm happy for you, Tate."

"Thank you," he said, and Alyson squirmed under the intensity of his gaze. He looked as though he was memorizing every detail of her being.

"Do you have siblings? Children?" she gently asked, feeling off balance and uncertain. She hated this formality between them but how the hell were you supposed to act when confronted with a former lover who belongs to someone else.

"No, on both counts. Vick had been pregnant but lost the baby late in the pregnancy. That was so difficult."

"That's heartbreaking. I'm so sorry."

"Thank you, Alyson," he softly whispered, reaching out to stroke her cheek with his fingers.

Alyson flinched at the intimate contact and looked away from him when he raised his eyebrows, silently questioning her response.

She cleared her throat and changed the subject. "Did you meet with Dr. Tucker before you left?"

"Yes I did. He said I had experienced dissociative fugue in response to the psychological trauma of witnessing the terrorist attack."

"I've never heard of that."

"I hadn't either but apparently my case was classic. Complete but reversible amnesia and the need to keep moving from one place to another."

"Does he expect you to relapse?"

"No. He said that now that my memories are back I should be fine. No treatment required."

"That's incredible, Tate. I'm so happy for you. I hope you never forget anything again."

"Thank you, Alyson. I'm pretty happy too. Next to my dad dying, the hardest part of this journey has been leaving you."

She could feel his eyes on her as she visibly swallowed, "We knew that was a possibility."

"That's true but it doesn't make it any easier to accept. I'd like to stay for a few weeks and spend some time with you, if that's okay? I'd love it if you would return to New York with me in a couple of months."

Alyson, shook her head, disbelieving what she was hearing. "You have your old life back and I don't fit into that."

"Of course you do! You'll always fit into my life, even more so now that I know my life again. These weeks away from you I've spent all my time remembering every little thing we've shared. Every little detail about you. I've missed you and I want to be with you. "

She was shocked by his words. "How on earth can you say those things to me? You have a wife! Does she even know that you're here now?"

Tate looked at her in confusion but then a smile slowly broke over his handsome face. There it was, that incredibly sexy smile that made her heart pound and her toes curl.

"Oh my God. You don't know!"

"Know what?"

"I'm not married, Aly. Vicki is my ex-wife."

"What? No. You introduced her as your wife."

"I'm sorry. That night was a blur. We were married at the time of my disappearance but the reason I hadn't walked into that building that day was because I was on the phone with Vicki and she was upset that I signed the divorce papers, even though she was the one who filed. She told me she didn't love me anymore and the truth was, I didn't love her either. We had gotten married out of some sense of duty to do right by the child she was carrying. When we lost the baby, we had nothing left to hold us together. She filed the papers after my disappearance. She's remarried with kids now."

"What? Really? You could have led with that! I spent the last two months believing you were married. Imagining you with her."

"Oh baby I am so sorry. Like I said, that night was a jumbled blur and I guess I didn't connect the parts you heard and what was said after you left. I'm not married. I'm free. I'm so sorry for not making that clear sooner."

"You're not married," she repeated, disbelief and relief colliding as she processed this new information.

"Is that why you didn't answer my calls or return my messages?"

"Yes. I didn't want to intrude on your marriage. It felt wrong to stay in touch. Plus I was trying to get over you and move on."

"There is no marriage. Just a gaping hole in my life where you should be."

"Tate," she whispered, tears rolling down her cheeks.

"Please don't cry. We can be together. If that's what you want. It's what I want, more than anything."

"Your life is in New York. My life is here. We live in different countries."

"So?"

"Well don't you think that complicates things?"

"A little perhaps but it's just geography. You're worth working through a few complications. I have feelings for you Alyson. Huge, terrifying, exhilarating feelings. I want to be with you."

When she didn't say anything, he quietly asked, "What do you want?"

Alyson stared at him, a myriad of emotions welling up inside. She remained silent.

"Please talk to me. Tell me what you're thinking. We have to talk this through."

She took a deep breath, "I missed you so much. It was almost as difficult as losing Joe. The only thing that made it more bearable was knowing you were alive and well and happy."

"Oh baby. What a mess we've made of this, huh?"

"I don't think I could survive losing you."

"Aly, you're not going to lose me."

"You can't promise me that."

"You're right. I can't. And I shouldn't. But I've fallen in love with you and I can promise to be there for you until my last breath."

"I'm not sure if I'm strong enough or brave enough to try."

"You'd rather live your life alone?"

"I don't know. Maybe," she whispered.

Tate took a deep breath. "When I first met you I didn't feel worthy of you. I didn't have anything to offer you. You were kind to me. So accepting. I never felt that you were judging me, or my choices. I developed feelings for you. Immediately. I wanted you more than I have ever wanted a woman in my life. I knew we didn't have a shot because I had no idea who I was or what situation I'd be dragging you into with me."

"It didn't matter to me, Tate. I wanted you to have peace of mind but as for not having anything to offer me, all I wanted was you."

"And now that you know the full truth, something has changed for you. You don't want me anymore?"

"That's not true. Of course I want you. I thought you were someone else's and that was difficult to accept."

"May I hug you? Please?" he asked, looking unbearably handsome and vulnerable.

She nodded and he moved closer, pulling her into his arms. He held her tightly and she wrapped her arms around his back, returning his embrace. God he felt so good. She had missed him so much.

"I want to kiss you but I don't think I'll be able to stop at a kiss. I want you," he said as his lips brushed against her hair.

"Please," she whispered just before his mouth closed over hers. He kissed her as though he was dying of thirst and she was a desert oasis. They impatiently removed their clothing as they loved and marked and pleasured each other. They weren't gentle. They were raw and animalistic in their possession of each other. They didn't stop, couldn't stop, until they were weak from exhaustion. And then they started again.

EPILOGUE

Alyson was slowly waking from a dream. In that dream Tate had come to visit her. He had told her he wasn't married. He had made love to her repeatedly throughout the night and he had stayed with her for weeks. She didn't want to wake. She wanted to stay in that dream world where he could be hers. She smiled as strong arms tightened around her, pulling her close and warm lips pressed kisses against the curve of her shoulder. *Thank God. She hadn't been dreaming. He was real. They were together.*

"Good morning," he said, kissing her neck just below her ear.

"Good morning," she replied, pressing back against him, making him groan.

"Are you sore?"

"Very. You were an animal last night," she laughed.

"Take a bath with me," he invited. "The hot water will soothe you."

"Mmmm. I'd love that," she sighed.

He pressed a kiss against her shoulder and rolled out of bed. A moment later she heard the water running in the Jacuzzi of their bathroom on the fiftieth floor of Tate's favourite hotel in New York City. It was the same room he had stayed in his very first night back in New York all those months ago. She smiled as she thought of the ways he had changed since she had first met him. There was no cloud of uncertainty hanging over them. No fear of the unknown lurking around the corner. Tate was free in every sense. He had a newfound, or perhaps newly rediscovered, confidence. He was assertive without being overbearing. He was ambitious and filled with dreams. He didn't hold any part of himself back. Sexually he was attentive and had developed a newfound hunger and an inexhaustible drive. He also had a subtle command about him that excited her.

He walked back into the room and pulled the covers off her, revealing her naked body.

"God I want you again," he growled, trailing his fingers down her side and over her hip.

"You promised me a bath. First," she smiled. "Plus I want to brush my teeth."

"Okay, I suppose," he playfully grinned, offering her his hand to help her out of bed.

She loved this side of him. She had cared deeply for him as John but as Tate, he was irresistible. In the past three months, since he had returned, she had fallen deeply in love with him. She brushed her teeth while he stepped into the tub. He had turned the jets on and the bubbling water looked inviting. He looked inviting. As she approached him he once again offered her his hand and helped her step into the water, steadying her as she lowered her body to fit in the space between his parted legs, her back pressed against his chest.

"Feel good?" he asked.

"Incredible," she sighed, sinking lower into the steaming water.

"Dave is bugging me about us visiting them. He says it's been three months. That's not acceptable apparently."

Alyson laughed, "Does he know that this is my first trip to visit you?"

"Yes. But he's relentless."

"Well how about next weekend? Instead of flying back to Newfoundland we could head west."

"Yeah? That would be perfect. I can't wait for them to meet you. They're going to love you, Aly."

"I hope so. Otherwise you'll have to ditch me."

"Not a chance."

"I'm loving this room but I'm looking forward to going back to your place tonight."

"Me too but I had to fulfill my fantasy of having you in this room."

"It's been the best night of my life so far. Until tonight back at your place. Then that will be the best night of my life so far."

"God I love you."

"I love you, too."

"You know I don't think of that apartment as my place. It's temporary. The lease will expire in a couple of months. Maybe you can help me look for a more permanent place while you're here."

"That sounds like fun. I'd love that. When's your meeting with the developers again?"

"Not until Friday morning. We will be visiting three potential sites for the housing project."

"I'm so happy you were able to revive your dream to build those housing units."

"Me too, baby," he said, nuzzling her neck.

Alyson smiled as he wrapped his arms around her and held her tight. She was enjoying the soothing heat of the water and being so close to Tate.

"Did I tell you about my list?"

"What list? For the housing project?"

"No. My "to do" list. The housing project is on it but there are lots of other things on there, too."

"Oh? Like what?" she asked, turning her head to look up at him.

"I want a family of my own, Alyson. That's near the top of my list."

Alyson paused for a moment, carefully choosing her words, "You've missed out on fifteen years of your life, Tate. I think wanting a family would be a realistic priority."

"Ask me what's at the top of that list," he softly directed, his eyes holding her gaze had suddenly turned serious.

Alyson's heart was pounding as she asked the question, "What's at the top of your list, Tate?"

He gently turned her to face him, pulling her onto his lap so that she was straddling him in the water.

"You Alyson. I want you more than anything. Anyone."

"I want you too."

He pulled her forward, impaling her on his hardness. Her moan filled the room.

"Marry me, Alyson. Be mine. Forever. Make babies with me."

She braced her hands on his shoulders and fought to maintain clarity as he wreaked havoc on her body and her mind with his skillful ministrations beneath the water.

"You're serious?" she asked, as he pulled her harder against him, moving deeper inside of her.

"Yes. I want you to be my wife. I want to be your husband. Say yes."

"It's so soon, Tate," she moaned as he slowly made love to her, his gaze holding hers.

"It's not soon enough. I want you next to me every day. We can split our time between here and Newfoundland. Or we can stay there. I don't care where we are as long as we're together. Marry me. Say you'll marry me."

She thought of the lonely hours she had endured after he had left in November. She thought of how deeply she had missed him and longed for him. She remembered how empty and heartbroken she had felt thinking she had lost him forever. They had been inseparable since he showed up at her house in late January and she knew in her heart she couldn't return to Newfoundland without him. She looked into his eyes, his incredible jade green eyes and let love guide her.

"I don't want to live without you, either."

He stilled and his hands moved to cup her face, "Is that a yes?"

"That's a yes," she laughed.

He swelled and surged inside of her, leaving them both breathless.

"Soon Alyson. I want to marry you soon."

"God, yes," she sighed, as he showed her how thoroughly he would love her every day from now on.

THE END

Made in the USA
Columbia, SC
06 September 2017